I0548206

RHODES

BOOK FOUR OF THE ANGELBOUND OFFSPRING SERIES

CHRISTINA BAUER

COPYRIGHT

Monster House Books
Newton, MA 02135
ISBN 9781946677341
Second Edition

Copyright © 2019 by Monster House Books LLC
All rights reserved. This book or any portion thereof may not be reproduced
or used in any manner whatsoever without the express written permission of
the publisher except for the use of brief quotations in a book review.

CONTENTS

DEDICATION

For All Those Who Kick Ass, Take Names
And Read Books

COLLECTED WORKS

Angelbound Offspring

The next generation takes on Heaven, Hell, and everything in between

1. Maxon
2. Portia
3. Zinnia
4. Rhodes
5. Kaps
6. Mack
7. Huntress

Angelbound Origins

About a quasi (part demon and part human) girl who loves kicking butt in Purgatory's Arena

1. Angelbound
2. Scala
3. Acca
4. Thrax

5. The Dark Lands
6. The Brutal Time
7. Armageddon
8. Quasi Redux
9. Aquila

Angelbound Lincoln

The Angelbound experience as told by Prince Lincoln

1. Duty Bound
2. Lincoln
3. Trickster
4. Baculum
5. Angelfire

Fairy Tales of the Magicorum

Modern fairy tales with sass, action, and romance

1. Wolves and Roses
2. Moonlight and Midtown
3. Shifters and Glyphs
4. Slippers and Thieves
5. Bandits and Ball Gowns
6. Evil Queens and Goblin Kings

Pixieland Diaries

Sassy pixie Calla loves elf prince Dare. Too bad he hasn't noticed her. Yet.

1. Pixieland Diaries
2. Calla
3. Dare
4. Ley Queen

Dimension Drift

Dystopian adventures with science, snark, and hot aliens

1. Scythe
2. Umbra
3. Alien Minds
4. ECHO Academy

This is a completed series.

Beholder

Where a medieval farm girl discovers necromancy and true love

1. Cursed
2. Concealed
3. Cherished
4. Crowned
5. Cradled

This is a completed series.

RHODES

ZINNIA

I may be a princess trapped in a tower, yet I am a happy one. Why? My Rhodes sits nearby, strumming a new rhythm on his acoustic guitar.

Ah, sweet music.

The tower itself is called the Dragon's Claw, for it resembles a huge talon that arcs up from ground. All around it, red desert stretches off in every direction.

Yes, it is a prison.

Happily I am on good terms with the warden, who is my sister, Huntress. My parents placed me and my sisters in this tower—that means Kaps is here as well—along with specific instructions for Huntress. Mum and Da trust her judgment. When Huntress tells the guards to look the other way, that's what happens. Tonight, Huntress ordered the tower's rooftop terrace to be vacated. Now I may enjoy *alone time* with my fated mate, what we dragon shifters call our *rhana*.

It is much appreciated.

Leaning back on my lawn chair, I stare up at the night sky.

My Rhodes plays on. The new tune wraps about my soul. Staccato notes pluck at my heart. Long chords follow, moving into a slow refrain that captures Rhode's inner strength. The song ends. I sigh.

"That was lovely. "

"Thank you."

With the tune ended, I refocus on Rhodes once more. He is tall and lean with whip-strong muscle. While I've been in the Dragon's Claw, my Rhodes has been training to join the Kathikon, the Emperor's Guard. The work has paid off. My rhana's shoulders, arms, and legs now bulge with muscle. His brown hair is cropped short; I long to run my fingers across the shorter cut. He fixes me with his moss-green eyes.

How long have I just been staring at him? Too long, possibly.

I clear my throat. "I've no lyrics for you yet."

"Not a worry. I know you'll come up with something lovely."

Usually, I must hear a new tune at least three times before lyrics appear. These first listens are the best, though. I am not torturing myself to find the right phrase or rhyme. The song simply moves through me.

"Please play it again and soon," I say.

"Happy to oblige."

My Rhodes grins, and his long lashes add extra emphasis to any expression. The sight makes my heart spark. Turning, he resets his guitar into its case. This is a careful business, by the way. My Rhodes worked hard to rebuild one of his old childhood instruments. Now, any scratch on that guitar would feel like a deep wound to both of us.

While my Rhodes finishes his work, I soak in my surroundings once more. The roof terrace holds little.

Huntress, Kaps, and I dragged up a trio of lawn chairs. That's about it. My parents say we must live here for our safety, yet they give few specifics. Mum and Da rarely visit, so we've had little chance to get more information.

That's when I notice something new.

"Is that a picnic basket?" I ask.

My Rhodes carefully closes his guitar case with a small click. "It is."

I spent years being held by the Triumvirate on Earth. During that time, my sole source of nutrition was dried protein bars. When I first escaped, I tried all sorts of foods. That didn't end well. Now I only eat plain burgers. My Rhodes has been worried. He wishes to expand my diet.

My Rhodes opens the basket. Small containers line the interior. "I brought things we can taste together."

On reflex, my mouth scrunches into a frown of disgust. "There is no forgetting the last thing I tried."

"Dried chili peppers are not meant to be eaten by the handful."

I count off more culinary disasters. "Or pickles. Or salt. Or cinnamon. The things eaten here are disgusting. I like my burgers."

My Rhodes shoots me a sly look. He knows that after that song, I'll do just about anything he asks. "How about this?" He opens a small container and takes out a little red thing.

"Is that bloody? I won't eat anything that drips blood."

"It's not bloody. It's a strawberry."

Vague memories sift through the back of my mind. I recall my life as a child, before I was taken by the Triumvirate. Sunshine spilled out over a bowl of red fruit topped with cream. *Strawberries. Delicious.* Sitting upright and sideways on my chair, I reach toward the fruit and stop myself.

Delicious, my foot. I also thought that about the dried chili peppers.

My Rhodes sits down beside me on the lawn chair. He holds up a strawberry and pops it in his mouth. "Mmmmm." Then, he offers another one to me.

I scooch away from him an inch. "Still looks bloody."

My Rhodes chuckles. I love the way the moonlight outlines his strong frame as his shoulders shake with laughter. "I've an idea." My Rhodes reaches into the basket and pulls out a long checkered napkin. "Cover your eyes and you won't see a thing."

I am Furor. Our powers cover the mortal sins of lust and wrath. At this suggestion, something stirs inside me. All of a sudden, I can't think of anything I want more than to have my eyes covered while My Rhodes does anything. I'd even try more chili peppers if he asked.

"All right." My heart thuds faster against my rib cage.

With gentle movements, my Rhodes rolls the napkin into a band that he ties over my eyes. "Comfortable?"

I nod. To be honest, I'm perhaps a little intrigued here.

All right, far more than a *little* intrigued.

"Ready for your first taste?" asks my Rhodes. His voice is the perfect mixture of growly and sweet.

"Yes."

I open my mouth and my Rhodes sets a round something on my tongue. I try to speak past the shape, but it's not easy. "Isth bumpy."

"Those are tiny seeds. They don't taste like anything. You need to bite down to get the real flavor."

What kind of taste will I find?

I test the item out on my tongue. It certainly doesn't have the coppery tang of blood. Little by little, I bite down. The flavor bursts with the sweetness of summer. I chew quickly and swallow. "I remember! Huntress, Kaps, and I ate these when we were little! Great bowls of strawberries and cream!"

"Ready for another one?"

"Oh, yes." I open my mouth. This time, my Rhodes sets something hard and flat on my tongue. I bite down right away. It is starchy and salty. "Not bad."

"That's a cracker. Ready for another?"

I merely open my lips in reply. My Rhodes pops a small square in my mouth. I bite down into the most glorious flavor ever. It is smooth and sweet, creamy and dark, all at once. I stop chewing so I may savor the taste. Without meaning to, a single sound escapes me. "Mmmm."

"That, my lovely Zinnia, is chocolate."

With my right hand, I lift my blindfold up a little so I may shoot my Rhodes a sly look. With my left hand, I crook him closer. The meaning is clear.

Let's share.

RHODES

Zinnia wants to share a chocolate kiss? No need to ask me twice.

Cupping her face in my palms, I lean in until our mouths touch. Once our tongues meet, I taste the sweet chocolate. Fire ignites inside me. It's been three long months since Zin and I battled Chimera. In all that time, I've lived in a barracks with other warriors. And Zin has been locked up here. I see her for an hour every month or so.

Who knows when our next time will be?

I deepen the kiss and flip onto my back. Zin sits astride me. She's everything fierce and lovely with her bright eyes and long pale dreads. She runs her hands under my shirt. Her petal-soft skin teases against the hard planes of my chest.

This is agony.

This is everything.

A knock sounds on the round wooden panel set into the floor. It serves as a makeshift door to the roof terrace. "Zin?"

I know that voice. It's Zin's sister, Huntress.

Damn.

Zin breaks our kiss. We share a long gaze that mixes longing, joy and despair. "What is it, Huntress?"

"You've got two minutes," says Huntress.

"Got it." Zin leans down to kiss me again.

Huntress' voice sounds again. "Rule 17. No romance in the tower." The emperor and empress gave Huntress a set of so-called *tower rules*. She's sticks to them like scales onto a dragon's hide.

"Can we bend that rule more than break it?" asks Zin.

"Already done," says Huntress.

I tap Zin's shoulder. "We better sit up. Huntress doesn't like enforcing these rules any more than we like living by them."

Huntress' voice echoes through the wooden panel once again. "Thank you, Rhodes."

I wrap my arm around Zin's shoulder and take care to speak in an extra-loud voice. "For warmth, not romance."

Zin chuckles. "Agreed."

"I have a confession to make," I whisper.

"This sounds serious." Yet the way Zin bobs her brows, she knows it isn't at all grave.

"I came here to distract us both."

Zin taps her chin while scrunching up her forehead. It's her way of thinking things through. "From the fact we haven't played music in a while?"

"No."

"From your training?"

"Not worried about that."

"Neither am I." The playful look on Zin's face fades. "You don't mean Killian's trial?"

Months ago, the emperor and empress captured Killian, the Triumvirate leader. He'll be brought to trial. In Furonium, that means that the empress will receive a magical vision about his guilt or innocence.

Right.

Let's face it, since Killian kidnapped the empress' daughter, there isn't a lot of wiggle room here. "I don't think Killian will be found innocent." I take Zin's hands in mine. "I'm worried about you. Huntress tells me you aren't sleeping."

Zin raises her voice. "Huntress is a blabbermouth."

"She's your sister and she loves you."

Zin narrows her eyes. "So that's why you were allowed to visit?"

"It is."

"I'll have nightmares more often if it means I get chocolate kisses."

I move closer until our foreheads touch. Zin is all things brave and lighthearted. Still, it tears at me, thinking that she carries awful burdens inside. "Please. It might help to talk about it."

Zin lifts her chin. "Killian lied to me. He kidnapped me and claimed I was the last dragon shifter alive. H even said it was an honor for me to become possessed by Chimera's ghost. For years, I lived in a cave with nothing but protein bars to eat and battle training to keep my mind busy. And now, the rumors are that Killian wants to challenge you to marry me. It's beyond words."

A satisfied grin rounds my mouth. "That's my fighting Zinnia. But I don't think that's what's keeping you awake at night." Zin's shoulders slump. That's as close to a confirmation as I'll get. "What has you so sad?"

"Nothing saddens me about the Triumvirate."

"I didn't say the Triumvirate was the cause of your sorrow, Zinnia."

A long pause follows before Zin speaks again. "When we first met, I could tell you things. Back then, I thought I was the Vessel of Chimera. Whatever burdens I carried, I wouldn't hold them for long. It is different now." She sighs, and there's no missing how her voice quivers with sorrow. "I know you're my rhana and I should tell you everything. Yet on this, I have no words."

"Take your time, Zin. When you find the words, I'll be here."

Zin gives me the side eye. "Well, not *right* here. I am a dragon princess locked up in a tower."

"Give the word to Huntress and I'll be over as quickly as I can." I brush the softest of kisses against her lips. I wish we could set up direct communications, but that goes against the tower rules. "All right?"

"Yes." Zin smiles.

"Good."

Zin and I have an understanding. No long good-byes. When our time is up, I leave and quickly. Rising, I step over to the tower's edge. Pulling on my inner shifter power, I summon my magic. Green light emanates from my skin. Soon a sheath of emerald brightness surrounds me. When it vanishes, I am a great green dragon. Leaping from the tower's edge, I take off into the night sky.

Even though I don't look back, I sense my rhana watching my every move.

3

ZINNIA

a night breeze tangles my sundress around my legs as I watch my Rhodes fly away. All too soon, there is no discerning him from the rest of the night sky. Turning about, I stare at the round plank set into the floor.

"Huntress, are you still there?" I ask.

In reply, the wooden disc slides aside. Huntress pops her head up through the opening the floor. Her violet eyes gleam in the starlight. Long brown hair tumbles down her shoulders. "What do you need?"

That's Huntress for you. She's the silent glue that keeps things together. Most teenagers would be whining that they have to play babysitter to their sisters. Huntress does her duty.

"I've a question, if you've a minute," I reply.

Huntress climbs up onto the roof. She kicks at the floor. "The tile here needs re-grouting. It's falling apart. I'll alert the servants."

"You don't have to do that, Huntress."

"If I don't, who will?"

I shrug. "Grout is over-rated. And what kind of word is *grout*, anyway?"

"In other words, no one will fix the tiles until some unfortunate falls." She looks to me. "Come now. I'm not here to chat about flooring. What troubles you?"

I open my mouth, ready to share. In fact, I had big plans for this moment. Now that Huntress is here, I can't seem to get out the words.

"Let me guess, then." Huntress folds her arms over her chest. "It's about breathing fire."

Both Kaps and I were born into the Firelord tribe, which means we should be able to breathe flame. Neither of us can. Kaps never wanted to learn. In my case, I was forbidden from developing the skill. Quite wisely, the Triumvirate figured I'd escape if I spout flame. "I'm not anxious about that."

Huntress frowns. "But Mum and Da haven't approved Rhodes as your rhana. Other dragons could fight him for your hand. And since you can't breathe fire, any dragon could try. Even Killian could lay a claim."

"Killian." The name feels like acid on my tongue. "How is he walking free?"

"Mum and Da have their reasons." Huntress holds up her hands, palms forward. "I don't know their justification, mind you. But I wouldn't be so certain Killian won't try to fight Rhodes."

"Agreed."

At this point, Huntress and I would normally launch into a conversation about breathing fire. I would ask Huntress for lessons. She'd say that's against the rules. I'd counter that if I could breathe fire, then it would put Killian off his pursuit. And in truth, it is tempting to retread that familiar ground.

But it is not why I asked Huntress here.

Focus, Zinnia.

I take in a long breath. "My ability to breathe fire is certainly a point of anxiety. It is not one that worries me now."

Huntress moves closer. "Then what is it, my sister?"

"There was someone…" Sorrow burns through me. My eyes sting with tears. "One of the Triumvirate." With every ounce of strength inside me, I want to speak her name.

Gracie.

She was both mother and friend … confidante and teacher. When Gracie was murdered, I only felt numb. Looking back, that was the easy time. Now mourning her is so much harder. I'm desperate to find more Triumvirate members like Gracie. I know it won't bring my dear friend back. Even so, the thought won't leave my mind. I've even come up with a plan.

I straighten my shoulders. "I wish to find a private investigator on Earth."

"To find this member of the Triumvirate?"

"Or others like this person. You serve as the Enforcer of the Realm. Mum and Da send you to Earth on all sorts of missions. If anyone can find me a private investigator, you can."

"It would help if I knew your full plan."

This part is rather vague. All I wish is to connect with Gracie's people. Once I do that, I shall find a way to help them. It could help repay my debt for the way Gracie aided me.

How do I explain that to myself? To anyone?

I shake my head. "I do not have the words."

Huntress stares off over the desert for a moment. She nods to herself and then looks back to me. "There is only one private investigator to choose. I'll send out some messages. Prepare to sneak away from the tower tomorrow night. You'll only be gone a few hours. No luggage."

I exhale. I've spent months agonizing over this plan. Knowing I may be meeting an actual private investigator soon? It's as if lead weights were pulled from my shoulders.

"Do we meet at the upper basement?" I ask.

"That's how Kaps sneaks off," says Huntress. "And it's well watched. No, if you're leaving, it must be absolutely secret. I'm breaking at least five rules for you."

"Thank you."

"We're sisters," says Huntress. "Watching out for each other is what we do." She steps over to the hole once more. "We'll meet right here. Tomorrow. Midnight." She pauses. "You did not tell Rhodes anything about this." Again, it's not a question.

"I did not." *Although I wish I could have.*

"Ah." Huntress nods slowly. "I understand." Her violet eyes glint in the starlight.

"You do?"

"Yes, because…" She pauses, searching for what to say. When she speaks again, Huntress' voice is low and gentle. "Because of how I came to be your sister."

A realization washes over me. Huntress' tribe, the glass dragons, would not serve the evil emperor Chimera when he was alive. As punishment, her realm was destroyed. As far as we know, Huntress is the only survivor.

My poor sister.

Without another word, Huntress steps off into the darkness and is gone.

Seems I'm not the only one who doesn't like chatting about terrible things.

I press my hand against the wooden slats of my lawn chair. A little warmth remains from where my Rhodes and I laid together and kissed. I check the rooftop for his basket and guitar. Both vanished with his magic, as expected.

I won't allow him to disappear from my life as well.

4

RHODES

THE NEXT DAY

*A*nother day, another practice fight in the Octodrome. I step onto the red earth of the battle octagon. Rows of empty benches rise up around me. The red sun of Furonium sears down from a cloudless sky. I thump my fist against the chest plate of my new body armor.

Solid fit.

This plating is not what I'm used to, but this is a new Kathikon school which is based on thrax-style training. Our empress' father happens to be the thrax king, so we got free advice on how to set up our own warrior academies. At first, everyone thought it was a joke. Now, we realize it's something else.

Brutal.

And also incredibly effective.

Two thin alleys cut through the stands surrounding the

octagon. My opponent could come through either one. Lately, I've been battling other warriors from my class and barracks.

A shadow moves in the passage to my right. I raise my trident high, ready to fight. Yet it isn't an opponent who steps onto the octagon. It's my uncle, Atlas. He's a slightly smaller version of my late father, which means Atlas is over six feet tall with green-tinted skin and hefty muscle in black body armor. He has a wide nose and a thin ridge of spines along his skull.

"Rhodes!" he calls. "Visitor."

I lower my trident. "Now?"

Atlas doesn't answer. He simply turns back into the access passage and disappears into the darkness. My last visitor was Bash, the drummer from our band, Cool Daze. It's the very same group that's been spiking on the human billboard charts for months. The reason? *Our Song*, a tune by me and Zinnia.

It's music my uncle would like to pretend never happened.

And it's all part of why I'm here, training to be a warrior like my father. My family hopes I'll become entranced by my father's legacy and forget my music and my rhana.

Not happening.

Ah, well. It's not like they can stop Bash from visiting. But it's odd to allow such a meeting during battle practice. Hoisting my trident over my shoulder, I step into the same access passage as Atlas. At the end, there's a looping hall that encircles the Octodrome.

My mother stands there. Sienna.

Some days, my mother is all glamour and performance. She used to be human celebrity in her own right. Sienna played the cello and regaled crowds with eccentric tales.

Today, she's a frail figure in a loose sheath dress. Her long gray braid is almost white now.

I tilt my head, wondering. Which Sienna will greet me today? The one who was thrilled when I survived a battle with Chimera? Or the one who's angry that I upset the natural order, love Zinnia, and place the imperial family at risk?

"Greetings, Sienna."

"Rhodes." She shakes her head. The movement sends her braid swaying.

It's to be angry Sienna today.

"There's a side room where we can chat," I state. Without waiting for a reply, I march down the hallway. Like the rest of the Octodrome, the place is made from black granite. I press open the door to find a snug room with dark walls and no decoration.

Sienna steps around in a slow circle. "This is rather empty."

"It's for warriors to warm up before entering the octagon." I lean against the wall and wait. Sienna has a point here. She'll get to it.

"According to Atlas, this is now the best training facility in Furonium."

"It is."

"Every swipe of the sword should help you remember your father's heritage."

"It does."

"Your father enjoyed music, but didn't let it cloud his duties."

Setting the pointed end against the floor, I twirl the trident in my fist. "Let me guess. You're here because Bash visited me last month. Of all people, you should know I can't cut music out of my soul."

A fire light's my mother's amber eyes. "This is about far more than music. Your father knew his place. He served in the royal palace. He didn't place the imperial family at risk by chasing after what wasn't his."

Protective energy surges through every muscle in my body. "Zinnia is my rhana. I brought her *back to life* during the battle with Chimera. How is this still a question?"

"Because she isn't yours until the emperor and empress give their blessing. You must prepare for the inevitable."

"Note taken."

Sienna shivers slightly. For her, inner frustration rises like water boiling. Soon, she'll spout her true purpose. Sure enough, she rounds on me once more.

"Why are you sneaking off to visit Zinnia anyway? Someone else could challenge you and ki—" Sienna pops her hand over her mouth.

So that's what this really is all about. *Losing me.*

Setting the trident aside, I march over and envelop my mother in a deep hug. It lasts all of three seconds, which is a record for us.

Sienna steps away. "Thank you, Rhodes. I'm fine now."

I gesture across my torso. "I'm a big bad warrior these days. No one beats me on the octagon. No one will defeat me in a challenge for Zinnia." I'd add that finding my rhana again has boosted my lightning powers, but that would only cause Sienna more questions and worry.

"Killian isn't just anyone," says Sienna. "I realize you and Zinnia have a rhana bond, but many people live full lives without one."

"I'm not worried about a blessing from the emperor and empress. They need time. So does Zinnia." After all, the emperor and empress just reconnected with their daughter after years apart. That's a lot to take in, even without the question of Zin finding her rhana.

"The longer a prince or princess waits to settle their marriage, the more dragons will fight over their wedding. Early marriage saves lives." She huffs out a breath. "I can't believe the emperor and empress have kept things calm for as long as they have."

"Zinnia only turned eighteen three months ago."

"Three months after Tempest turned eighteen, forty dragonesses were dead. All fought for the right to marry him. Emperor Tempest entered into a paper marriage with an eldress of the mammoth tribe. That held up for hundreds of years."

Which is old history. Everyone knows how Tempest married Buxom, a ten-story-tall elder dragoness. Mammoths never change out of their dragon forms. Buxom didn't much care when they were wed. She minded even less when the papers were torn up. Even so, the very concept of Zinnia marrying anyone but me makes my blood boil.

"Zinnia is not marrying some giant fur dragon. Not even for show."

Sienna throws up her hands. "Your father served in the royal palace; he didn't try setting up residence there. We need to think about the imperial family."

"What about you?" I ask. There's no question what this conversation is *really* about. "It's all right for you to love a son, you know."

"Don't be a sentimentalist." She flashes a bright smile. All of a sudden, the frail Sienna is gone, replaced by a human performance tornado. I can picture her in a nightclub, cigar in her teeth, playing her cello while regaling an audience with bawdy tales. "Did I tell you about the time I juggled scimitars with the Prince of Persia while riding a barge down the Nile? It was dusk; that's a very important part of the story."

I've seen this move before. It's Sienna's way of saying the conversation is over. My mother loves me and worries. One thing I learned one thing early, though: Sienna is no puppet. She won't show her feelings the way other mothers do. Instead, I try to enjoy what she *can* offer.

Resting my shoulder against the wall, I kick my right ankle across my left. "As a matter of fact, I'd love to hear that tale."

And turns out, it's a good one.

5

ZINNIA

THAT NIGHT

*E*scaping the tower is rather easy. Huntress gives me a magical cloak and I walk off. Once I'm far enough away, I transform into my dragon self and take to the skies. From there, I follow directions to a place called Coronado in the human realm of California. The spot is rather deserted, but perhaps that's because of all the gates and guards I just flew past.

Good things humans can't see dragons. I felt certain there were armed warriors at those gates.

In short order, I land before a simple white house that overlooks the ocean. It's two stories high with lots of windows. Once I change back into my two-legged form, I wear a skirt-suit. It's uncomfortable in the extreme, but it is what humans wear. I'm supposed to blend in.

At this point, I can't help but notice a number of fascinating things. First, the sidewalk. If I angle my head correctly, it seems to glisten in the sunlight. What is in concrete, exactly? Plus, the grasses here are so perfectly trimmed and neat, they hardly look real. Who would place fake grass around their home? And these high heeled shoes. What purpose do they serve, other than to match other human women? Maybe it is part of some female ritual where pain is enacted on your feet.

Not for the first time, I realize how growing up in a cave has limited my knowledge.

I'm so amazed by what I see, I hardly notice the front door swing open. A teenager with ebony skin and short white hair waits on the threshold. "Are you coming in?"

Her words snap me out of my thoughts. "Absolutely." I try to take a few steps and almost fall over. The girl already invited me in, so surely I do not need to participate in this ritualistic foot-pain any more. I kick off my shoes and step up to the door.

"Greetings." I bow slightly at the waist. "I am Zinnia."

"That you are." She steps inside. "Close up behind you."

Walking inside, I find an airy place with simple white furniture. It matches the outside of the house, except for one thing. Ashtrays are everywhere.

Gross.

The girl pulls out a fresh cigarette and lights up. "This is a disgusting habit. Never start."

I chuckle. "That's funny."

She exhales. "Lung cancer is funny?"

"No, I'm trying to smoke, in my own way. And by that I mean, I wish to breathe fire." I press my lips shut, hard. That was too much to share. This is a human, after all.

"Why don't you have a seat?" Good thing she didn't comment on the fire-breathing thing.

"Thank you." I try to get comfortable on the couch, but it isn't easy in this skirt. Am I flashing my nether regions to this woman? What do I do with my legs? In the end, I decide to sit cross-legged and pile up pillows around me. That way my hiked-up skirt doesn't show. *Perfect.*

"You done?" asks the woman.

"Yes, thank you."

"I'm Jade Brooch."

"Nice to meet you. I'm Zin E. Ah. That's what it says on the song's liner notes, anyway."

"Both of us use false names, then." Jade tilts her head. "How do you know Huntress?"

"She's my sister."

Jade's brows raise. "Huntress is *your* sister?"

"In all the ways that count, yes."

"I don't mean to be rude." Jade takes a seat across from me. She wears a white jumpsuit. How can someone with such an affinity for white spend all her day smoking? It's a riddle, certainly. And did I mention it smells disgusting? It does.

I nod toward her cigarette. "Do you mind putting that out?"

"Smells extra bad to you, then?"

No point sugar-coating this. "Yes."

Jade extinguishes her smoke. Instead she takes to drumming her fingers on the small white side table beside her. All the while, I can almost picture the wheels of her mind turning. "You're a shifter like Huntress."

"And you're human."

"One hundred percent. Eighteen years old, same as you."

"I know another woman who was aware of shifters. Her name is Nikki. She drove our metal wagon about. How do you know about our kind?"

"You don't work for long in my business without running across the true nature of reality."

"And what do you think of it all?"

"I've adjusted." She starts to pick up a fresh smoke and stops herself. "Why are you here?"

"I was kept by a group on Earth."

"Let me guess. You're a dragon, so not many could hold you. I'm guessing it was the Triumvirate. They're a para-military group run by Thorntails, who are the serving class in your world. The good Thorntails were turned into nasty trouble-makers by an evil king." She snaps her fingers, trying to remember the name.

"Emperor Chimera," I state.

"That's the one. I've had dragon shifters in here before, asking about the Triumvirate. Normally, the converastion involves breaking a lot of stuff and screaming." She keeps drumming her fingers on the tabletop. "You're not upset, though. That means know someone in the Triumvirate. Someone you like."

"Correct."

"And your person is deceased."

"Yes." I rearrange my pillows and try not to make eye contact. It's uncomfortable, how much Jade sees. "She saved me."

"What do you know about the Triumvirate?"

"One of them was my friend." The next word stays stuck on my tongue. But I've come this far, I have to push it out. With a force of will, I speak her name out loud. "Gracie. She was my teacher."

Jade nods. "There are the three levels of the Triumvirate: Thorntails, warriors, and servants. They're also called the first, second, and third estates. Your friend must have been in the third category."

My breath catches. "You said servants. There were more than just Gracie?"

"Yes, there used to be many like her. They do more than teach, though. Essentially, the third estate runs the place."

My heart feels so light, it's as if I could soar on the power of my own joy. "Gracie helped me. I want to find out more about her and the third estate."

"And you want me to find information about her role in the third estate?"

"That's right. Maybe Gracie has family there. I wish to help them in any way I can, just like she helped me."

Leaning back, Jade kicks her feet forward. She wears flip-flips and has lovely pink toenail polish. "There are six good reasons why I can't take this case."

"I have money," I offer.

Jade shoots me a sad smile. "That isn't one of the reasons."

"Then what is?"

"First, the Triumvirate are incredibly secretive. Second through sixth, the second estate are brutal killers." She doesn't seem too upset about that fact, though. As a warrior, you can tell when someone else enjoys a good fight. That's Jade.

"You're refusing me, then?"

She chuckles. "You know I'm not." She slides a pad of paper closer and lifts up a pen. "What can you tell me?"

"Gracie and I lived in the desert near the last Trance-a-

Dance concert. There was a cave. She was killed nearby." I wince. "It's not much to go on."

"On the contrary," says Jade. "That's more than I usually get. My fee is five thousand each day plus expenses. Can you pay human money?"

"Rhodes and I have a new single on the charts. I can pay."

"Good." She opens a drawer, fishes around inside it, and pulls out a c-shaped arc of silver metal. "This is a wrist cuff. It will light up when you need to contact me. Dial 213-555-1212. Can you remember that?"

"I can." Huntress said I shouldn't linger once my business was done. "If there's nothing else you need, I must take my leave."

"One last question. That single you spoke of. There's another person on it. I heard rumors about him, too."

"Rhodes." I can't help but smile as I say his name.

"Does he know you're here today?"

"No," I reply.

"Isn't he your fated mate? I mean, what you call a..." She snaps her fingers again. "A rhana?"

"He is. I should tell him everything. I don't." I rise and step toward the door. We say our goodbyes, but I'm only half paying attention.

As I leave, another thought hits me.

It's not that I *won't* tell Rhodes.

I just *can't*.

6

RHODES

THREE WEEKS LATER

I lay on my bunk and try to sleep.

Emphasis on the word *try.*

My bed is jammed in a long barracks filled with rows of identical cots. Ninety-eight Furor recruits sleep here. Mostly, they wear us out so much all day that we could sleep on a bed of nails.

Or in my case, beside a buzz saw.

That's what it means to be bunked next to Gams. He's a stringy guy who's jammed with magic. Hexenwing tribe. None of us can use our powers here, though. Otherwise Gams could cast a spell to shut his snoring mouth.

Like I said, most nights it doesn't bother me.

This isn't most nights.

Tomorrow is Killian's trial.

I'll be there as a fact witness, considering how I saw Killian interact with Zin first hand. What a monster. Killian insisted

Zin was part of some voluntary camp. All the while, the old Thorntail had been holding her in the desert until my rhana could become the vessel for Chimera's soul.

Not that I'm likely to be called to testify. This is the Empress' show. She gets visions and makes her call. That's how justice in Furonium works. A realization snaps me out of my thoughts.

The barracks is utterly silent.

Hoisting myself up onto my elbows, I scan the long room. Pale beams of moonlight shine though the small square windows lining the walls. Of the ninety-eight recruits, precisely twenty-seven now stand up. They all have one thing in common.

Thorntail tribe, same as Killian.

But are they also part of the Triumvirate? It can't be possible for recruits in my own barracks to be allied with Chimera. The Triumvirate are dead. Or at the least, dying out. That's why they wanted to revive Chimera in the first place. And Zinnia destroyed Chimera in our last battle.

These Thorntails must be getting ready to serve. That's what they do, after all. It's been tough forcing them to learn fighting techniques. Their tribe is more likely to hand out supplies or straighten a bunker. Thorntails don't see it as demeaning to serve others. It's part of their daily meditation on life.

I lay back onto my pillow. That must be it. Someone must need Thorntail assistance.

"You can't make a claim if you're dead," rumbles a voice.

A sinking feeling rolls down my insides. Little by little, I go back up on my elbows. Perhaps I heard that wrong.

"What did you say?" I ask.

A brawny Thorntail steps forward. That's Io. It's short for Iota, but Io works better. After all, the guy is the size of a small moon, and the *real* Io spins around Jupiter.

"You can't make a claim if you're dead, Rhodes," repeats Io.

That sinking sensation turns downright nauseating. No Thorntail would stand up in the middle of the night to cause trouble unless a higher-up demanded it. Their new tribal lord is loyal to Tempest and Portia.

So who asked for this?

Io stalks closer. The floor rumbles a bit with each step. "What do you say about *that*, guard dog? Still want to sneak past the master's gate ... and mate with his bitch?"

Rage electrifies every nerve ending in my body. I leap up to standing. "No one speaks about Zinnia that way."

The Thorntails rush me as a group.

Fine.

I'm Electrophus tribe. That means I wield lightning the way Firelord dragons breathe flame. For months, I've been unable to fight with all my powers. All the while, my abilities have been growing as my protective instincts surge toward Zinnia.

Time to tap my inner energy.

I raise my arms so they're parallel with the floor. Inside, I pull on my Electrophus power. Lightning energy churns through my limbs. Keeping my arms straight, I clap my hands before me. Heavy lines of electric current bursts from my fingertips. The many cords twist to form a greater rope of crackling power—a vortex of lighting that careens down the main aisle of the barracks.

I pause, waiting for the Thorntails to get the hint. They

don't. In response they pull out daggers and short swords as they close in.

All right then.

I open my arms.

The lightning breaks loose.

Bolts split off from their main channel. I command each one to its target. Twenty seven lightning bolts. Twenty-seven Thorntails. They don't stand a chance.

Moving as one, the Thorntail dragons crumple to the ground. They're in pain now, but they'll recover. My power keeps them incapacitated.

The front door bursts open. Atlas' outline stands framed in the doorway. "Rhodes!" he cries. "Stop!"

I lower my arms. The bolts vanish. That display of lightning just broke about a hundred rules, but I don't care. They attacked me and called Zinnia a bitch. Those Thorntails are lucky to be breathing.

Atlas points in my direction. "You," he calls. "With me."

I follow Atlas out the door and into his private cabin. The place holds a single cot and a small desk. Once we're both inside, Atlas slams the door shut before rounding on me. His barrel chest heaves as Atlas tries to keep his cool. It's not working too well.

"What were you doing?" Atlas' hands curl to fists.

"Io said I couldn't be Zin's rhana if I were dead. He had friends with knives."

"And they're all Thorntails. You're much more powerful. You had no business—"

"That's right. They're *Thorntails*. Who gave them orders, Atlas? The new tribal chieftain is loyal to Tempest and Portia."

Atlas pauses. His jaw grinds as he thinks through this news. "And Killian is in court tomorrow."

"Which means there are more important things happening here. Tempest and Portia need to know about this."

Atlas paces a line before the door. Long seconds pass before he answers. "You're right. I'll take a message to emperor and empress."

"Great." I step over to the trunk at the foot of Atlas' bed. "Got anything I can wear? I can't meet the emperor and empress in pajamas."

"You won't visit the palace, Rhodes. In fact, you're lucky not to be in the brig. Hell, you still may end up there."

"Promise, promises." I wink.

"Keep your ass in my cabin. I'll bring your news to Tempest and Portia. Whatever you do, don't fry up any more Thorntails."

Now, I loathe the idea of Atlas seeing the emperor and empress without me, but I do understand the logic here. I must be seen as enduring some kind of punishment. Blasting up my barracks and then skipping off to the palace for a chat wouldn't do much for morale.

"I'll stay put." I raise my hand. "I won't like it, but I'll stay put."

"Gracious of you." My uncle turns toward the door.

"And Atlas?"

"Yeah?" He pauses and looks toward me again.

I fix him with a serious stare. "Thank you."

"You're a crazy *son of a gun,* you know that right?"

"So was Titan." Which is true. One of the reasons Sienna stopped touring was because Titan lost his ever-loving mind any time a heckler started up.

Atlas steps closer. "Tell me. That lightning strike against the Thorntails. How long did it take you to draw up that much power? An hour, maybe?"

I glance around the room, thinking. "A few seconds. Nothing more."

Atlas claps his hands on my shoulders. "Titan would be proud."

And my uncle hums as he leaves the cabin.

7

ZINNIA

I march across the desert in my dragon form. The Dragon's Claw is no longer visible. Nothing but sand stretches off in every direction. I pause. A bone-deep sense of satisfaction seeps through me. This is the perfect spot.

Here I shall learn to breathe fire.

Swooping my scaly head over my shoulder, I call back to my sisters.

"Let us work in this place."

My sisters lumber up to wait nearby. Like me, they are all in their dragon shapes. I'm a great black beast with red plates jutting up along the line of my back and tail. Kaps' creature is smaller than mine, yet her scales are a lovely mix of black and violet. And since Huntress is a glass dragon, she is now invisible.

Kaps spreads out her great wings. "This is a pretty spot. Let's fly first before we get down to it."

"No," I state. "You are here to teach me the secrets of

breathing fire. Tomorrow is Killian's trial. If I can enter the court room with the ability to exhale flame, it shall be a great advantage. Killian can not challenge Rhodes for the chance to marry me. Suitors will be limited to only the Firelord tribe. "

I don't add in the even more important fact here. It took me three weeks of hounding Huntress for her to allow us to practice fire breathing at all. We can not do so inside the palace, as too much there is made from wood. And leaving for such a purpose? It breaks many of my parents rules.

Still, I wore down Huntress eventually. I am becoming quite good at it.

Kaps refolds her wings against her body. "Right." She drums her front talons into the ground. "Let me think."

A minute passes.

Two.

Three.

I sit back on my haunches. "Did you not take those—*what are they called again?*—Sunday Scion trainings?"

Kaps slips out her long forked tongue slowly across her lower jaw. This means she is thinking hard. "Every week."

"And did not the Aristocharre show you how to breathe fire?" This is a trainer shows young Firelords the art of flame. My handmaiden, Xiao, told me all about this.

"Hey!" Kaps rubs her front paws together. "That gives me an idea. Maybe we could ship my old Aristocharre in here. Have *him* give you lessons."

"We discussed this before," says Huntress. Or rather, her disembodied voice speaks. "Item fifty-one. No one enters the tower except those on the approved list. Mum and Da do not trust what Killian is up to. They wish us kept safe. Only approved visitors."

"What about Rhodes?" asks Kaps. "He's not on the approved list."

It is not very princess-like of me, but I stick out my forked tongue at Kaps. She should not bring up my Rhodes. I have enough trouble seeing him without her comments.

"All the more reason to respect the list otherwise," says Huntress. "And it says we should not be roaming the desert, period. So let's get on with it."

"Sure, absolutely," says Kaps. "This is happening. One thing first, though. Did I tell you how we were contacted by Abracadawn?"

I frown. "Abraca-what?"

"Abracadawn," answers Kaps. "It's only the biggest thing in human music. The thing is a fair, rave, and concert series all in one. Think of it as a musical circus on steroids that goes all night. The organizers reached out. Whenever our band wants a spot on the main stage, they'll make a place for Cool Daze."

"Let us focus on fire breathing," I state.

"Fine, fine. I just thought you'd be excited. You have a number one single worldwide."

Arcing my long neck, I rear back for a better look at Kaps. This is one of my favorite mannerisms as my dragon-self. *Instant perspective.* One fact becomes clear.

"You are stalling."

"I'm thinking," says Kaps. "There's a difference."

Yet this does not make any sense. "Do you not recall *anything* from your years in Sunday Scion? It was four hours every week, was it not?"

"I know how long it was," snaps Kaps. She moves so her scaly bum faces toward me.

"Ouch!" cries Huntress. "You stepped on my claw." Kaps

moves back to her previous position, but the incident does bring up a good question.

"Would you mind making yourself visible?" I ask Huntress. "It will make for fewer interruptions."

"That is logical." Huntress materializes beside us. The sight of her still makes me shiver. Huntress is a great dragon made from what appears to be clear liquid. If I look hard enough, I can see the vista of desert through her.

"You are a beautiful dragon, Huntress."

"Thank you." A look of sheer misery overtakes Huntress' clear eyes. It is not easy for my sister to be the last of her kind.

Huntress quickly changes the subject. "Let's return to this fire breathing," she declares. "If our sister can learn this skill, it would be most helpful. There is far too much concern about Zinnia's marriage."

Kaps huffs out a breath. "I'm of age, too. No one cares about marrying me."

I raise my chin. "Technically, I'm the oldest."

"Only by seventeen minutes," says Kaps.

"It's more than age," says Huntress. "Killian is the force behind all this. And sadly, that dragon is fixated on Zinnia."

Kaps drops her head. "Of course." Her eyes widen. "Oh, oh, oh! I have it. The Aristocharre has a little trick for remembering how to breathe fire. It's bad. B-A-D."

"Bad as in useless?" asks Huntress.

"No, B-A-D as in each letter stands for something," says Kaps. "First, there's B. That means *Breathe*. So you take in a deep breath."

"And then what?" I ask.

Kaps rolls her eyes. "You need to breathe first, silly."

I inhale and nod. *Breath taken.*

"Second, it's A for *Activate*. There's a little starter in your chest. When you activate it, there will be a series of clicks, almost like a tiny heartbeat. That means the fire is igniting." Kaps crawls closer. "Do you feel your starter activating?"

I scan every inch of my dragon's body. There's no beat except my own heart. Although I can't say this out loud; I still hold my breath. So I shake my head *no.*

Kaps sighs. "Then you aren't ready for the third step, D. That means you can *Discharge* your fire."

I shake my head once more.

"Give it a try anyway, will you?" asks Kaps. "Just open your mouth and exhale. Who knows? It may work."

I do as my sister requests. After all, she is the one who went to Sunday Scion class. I exhale, yet only air escapes my dragon's jaw. I keep my mouth open, just in case a little flame happens to escape.

Huntress leaps closer and peers into my mouth. "I see nothing." She turns to Kaps. "What did you do during Sunday Scion class?"

A dreamy look enters Kaps' dragon eyes. "I brought notes on dragon artifacts and put them inside my textbooks. It looked like I was reading with class, but I was really learning new stuff to find. So fun."

Huntress sits on her back haunches. "I am uncertain this is a profitable use of time." Her clear eyes flick toward me. "I should never have let you talk me into this."

"Just a little longer." I position my body onto all fours with my neck fully stretched. "Perhaps I need to lengthen myself first. That way, I can take in more air."

"That could be it," says Kaps. "There were tons of lessons on breathing."

So I try to breathe fire with my body stretched and contracted.

Sitting up and lying down.

Flying and stationary.

Nothing works.

After a few hours of this, I unhappily agree to return to our tower. My visit to Killian in the court house will take place tomorrow.

And I shall go there without the ability to breathe fire.

8

ZINNIA

THE NEXT MORNING

The morning of the trial, I awaken very early. That's why I'm not surprised when a knock sounds on my bedroom door. I look up from my writing desk.

"Greetings, Zinnia," says a voice through the door. That's Xiao, my handmaiden.

"And to you as well. Please come in."

Xiao steps into the room. As always, she wears a black suit with a bowler hat, just like the rest of the Firelord staff. She has a perfectly round face with high cheekbones. Long black hair cascades down her back. In her arms, she holds a little tray of burgers. There is also a small bowl of strawberries, my new favorite. Xiao stares at my desk.

"More books on fire breathing?" asks Xiao.

"Yes, but they aren't too helpful." I sigh. "I can see why dragons need Sunday Scion class to learn the art of flame. These books make no sense." I scan a nearby page. "It says here, *you must feel the fire. Breathe it in. Activate it. The flame will become as one with your heart.*"

Xiao frowns. "What does that mean?"

"My point exactly."

"So what are you writing, if you don't mind my asking?"

"I am copying passages from the books. Perhaps that will help me to understand what they mean."

"Sounds wise. Then again, you have always been a rather clever dragon." Xiao sets the tray down at the edge of my desk. "Do you need anything else from me?"

Killian's trial begins in a few hours. That fact makes me look at Xiao in a new light. "You are from the Thorntail tribe."

"I am."

"What do you think of …" I lower my voice to a whisper. "Killian?"

"Well…" Xiao shifts her weight from foot to foot. It is forbidden for us to discuss Killian with any of the staff, let alone one of the Thorntails.

Perhaps I pushed Xiao too far.

"I do not wish to place you in trouble," I add.

Xiao glances nervously at the door. "The trial is today, right?"

"It is."

"Then I will tell you this. Killian is the risk every Thorntail faces. Our gift can be our downfall."

"What do you mean?"

"Thorntails are unique as a tribe. Our will flows down from our leader. When the Emperor was Chimera, my people did terrible things. Some were never able to break free from his spell."

"But Chimera is dead. I killed him myself. That should have broken the spell."

All the blood seems to drain from Xiao's face. "Good luck today, Milady." She then rushes from the room so quickly, her movement is little more than a blur. My insides twist with worry. Something is wrong here, very wrong. I check my wrist cuff from Jade.

Nothing blinks or shines.

No answers there, either.

9

ZINNIA

*E*arly girl. That's who I am.

I'm the type who awakens early so I can scoop up all the protein bars before my handlers can steal them. I've only been a royal for a matter of months, but one thing makes me grouchy.

We royals are last to everything.

Right now, that means we're the final ones to enter the courtroom for Killian's trial. I peep around the corner of our waiting area to scan the chamber itself. The courtroom is a massive black space with vaulted ceilings. Huge carvings of past emperors and empresses sit along the side walls, all of them in their dragon forms. The long floor is covered in benches and cut through by a wide center aisle. Every seat is packed with Furor in their human form. No one wants to miss this trial.

A great red chair sits at the far end of the room. It's a crimson seat that's perched atop a dais.

That throne is for Mum.

Once she became Empress, Mum gained the power for accurate visions. She hears pleas of the accused and uses that magic to make her judgment. Plus, all of this happens while Mum's in a trance.

Now, I've never seen Mum in a trance before. In fact, I haven't seen much of her or Da since I returned to Furonium. My parents been zooming off across the after-realms, trying to find out what Killian is up to. I tried to explain the truth to them: since I killed Chimera, we don't need to worry about Killian. No response.

An image appears in my mind. It's Xiao, speeding from my room after I mentioned Chimera. Could that evil emperor still be alive somehow? It doesn't seem possible. Yet the itchy feeling under my skin tells me otherwise.

I set the thought aside. *Chimera is dead.*

Stepping closer, Da gently rests his hand on my shoulder. "Ready, little luv?" Like all of us, Da wears his formal best as a member of the imperial family. Today that means a black military-style suit with a purple sash from his shoulder to his hip. A thin golden circlet sits atop my father's head.

"I'm ready," I reply.

For our part, my sisters and I all wear dresses to match our dragons' scales. Mine is black with a red sash at the waist. Kaps dons a dress of black and violet. Huntress wears white. And Mum is draped in a long red velvet gown. My mother's pale hair is plaited into a braid that winds about her head.

What is Mum thinking at this moment?

The orchestra launches into a regal tune. That's our cue to enter the courtroom proper. As we enter, the loud chatter calms to a murmur.

We cross the space.

The front benches are reserved for imperials and those directly involved in the case. In this case, my family fills both of those criteria. We take our seats on the right-hand side of the room. Killian sits alone on the left. He's a looming figure, what with his huge forehead, bulging cheeks, and a mile-long chin. His small marble eyes stare with a predatory gleam. He meets my gaze and grins.

My hands curl into fists. I learned fighting techniques from this man. How much would I love to use them now? *Very much indeed.* It takes a force of will, but I glance away to check the nearby benches for Rhodes. After all, my rhana is a witness, too.

Sure enough, my Rhodes waits only a few rows behind me. Sienna and Atlas sit beside him. My rhana looks extra handsome in his long black military coat. A dark leather cap sits atop his head. He winks; all thoughts of Killian melt away. I blush.

Some threads of unease loosen inside me. *Rhodes is here. Everything will be fine.*

Mum ascends up the steps and takes her seat on the throne. She raises her hand; the room falls silent. "My dragons, justice in Furonium is swift and accurate. I, Empress Portia Phi Tau Xavionus Guritha Rixum, shall use my powers of divination to determine the righteousness of this case. Rise, citizen Killian."

Killian stands, a movement that shows off his slick grey suit. Kaps and I share a dark look. Why was he allowed to dress up? Killian should be brought forward in chains.

"Citizen Killian," states Mum. "You've been accused of plotting against this throne, kidnapping our daughter Xi Iota

Nu Alpha, and attempting an insurrection with the ghost of Emperor Chimera. How do you plead?"

"Not guilty," says Killian.

Mum's features stay unreadable. "Explain."

"I am Thorntail. My will is not my own. My consciousness remains tied to Chimera."

Gasps erupt from the crowd. Mum raises her hand once more. All falls quiet. "The crown is aware of this possibility," declares Mum. "Chimera was powerful enough to exist as a ghost before. It is possible he could have survived through to this day. Do you have any other defenses to bring before me?"

"No," Killian states. "Allow your powers to judge me as you will."

"So mote it be," says Mum.

Without making a conscious decision, my sisters and I have all moved closer together. Now we clasp hands as we wait. What will unfold with our mother?

Mum's eyes roll back into her head. An anxious silence fills the air. A net of phantom power whirls around the room, invisible yet undeniable. *Magic.*

Mum changes.

Violet light shines out from my mother's eyes, nose, and mouth. When she speaks again, it is as if a hundred versions of her were talking at once.

"I have heard your claim," says Mum. "And there is only one reply."

A long pause follows. Bands of anxiety tighten around my chest. All my sisters and I grasp our hands together more firmly.

This is it.

Here comes the moment where Killian gets what he

deserves for all my years of suffering. Mum will toss him into the deepest dungeon.

"You speak the truth, citizen Killian," says Mum. "Your will is not your own."

My body turns numb with shock. Mum says Killian is not guilty. He will go free. No dungeons. No justice. How can this be happening?

Mum continues. "Chimera's soul still exists, yet the location is hidden from our sight. "

My heart sinks. Mum is holding Killian innocent because he's being puppeteered by Chimera. That's what Xiao knew. It's why my trusted handmaiden sped from the room.

Chimera's soul lives. *Oh, no.*

"Killian is to remain free. This is our vision." When my mother straightens once again, all signs of magical light have vanished.

The vision is over. She's just Mum again.

Well, *just Mum* if your mother happens to be a magical Empress, but that's beside the point.

Her words echo through my head.

Killian is to remain free.

The words seem to bounce off my skull. Killian kidnapped me. Attacked our people. Almost killed Rhodes as well. And perhaps Killian is mentally bound to Chimera, but that doesn't erase all responsibility, does it? Plus, Killian never said what he did was wrong. How can this vision be right?

Mum rises to address the crowd. "My dragons, I thank you for your—"

"One more thing," interrupts Killian.

Mum narrows her eyes in Killian's direction.

"Zinnia is unattached. You and the emperor have given no blessing for her to marry. She does not breathe fire, so any tribe may battle for her hand. I wish to do so at the next full moon."

I gasp. Now I suspected Killian might do such a thing, but I figured it would be hard for him to fight Rhodes from a prison cell. And even if Killian did stay free, I never suspected he'd announce a challenge during his court trial. I glance between Mum and Da. Surely, one of them will tell Killian he is wrong. I could never be married to one such as him. Both my parents remain stony faced and silent.

I open my mouth, ready to declare the truth. *I have a rhana! Killian deserves prison!*

Huntress leans in to whisper in my ear. "Say nothing. Can't you see what's happening?"

Now, I do not see any logic here. Yet I trust Huntress. She can read politics in ways I can only guess at. It's why she's my parents' master spy and enforcer. So I wait.

Mum stays standing. "Until the next full moon. Court is dismissed."

The music sounds again. I walk out in a daze.

What just happened here?

10

RHODES

*T*hat did not just happen.

I did not sit in a courtroom and watch as the empress let Killian go. And even worse, she told that evil bastard he could battle for Zinnia's hand. Frustration heats my limbs.

That's not acceptable.

Not even close.

Killian grins in my direction. *Bastard.* Then he saunters down the main aisle and out the front door. What game is he playing at? And more importantly, why is he winning?

Atlas gently nudges me with his elbow. "We must leave, Rhodes. The empress has spoken."

I glare at my uncle. Every fiber of my being fires with white-hot rage. "No."

"Rhodes, you've already caused enough trouble for me in one week."

That catches my mother's attention. "Trouble?" asks Sienna. "What are you talking about?"

I raise my arm. An intricate web of lightning encircles my hand like a glove. Atlas's eyes widen. He's never seen this level of control over lightning. Focusing on my uncle, I speak three words in a low voice. "I'm going now."

I stalk off in the direction of Zinnia. *This isn't over.*

Atlas steps along at my side. "Where are you off to? Behind the courtroom, it's nothing but a maze of chambers. You won't find her."

"Take Sienna home," I state. "Make sure she's safe."

Speaking of Sienna, she steps into my path. "Take one more step toward the imperials, and you'll lose me."

Pausing, I shake my head. "You know better than to make a dragon choose against his rhana."

I move on.

Atlas and Sienna don't follow.

And as for some labyrinth behind the courtroom? Atlas should know better. We shifters have an enhanced sense of smell. I'll simply follow Zinnia's scent until I find her.

No matter how long it takes.

11

ZINNIA

My family and I walk out of the courtroom and into the antechamber beyond. Da rounds on us. "You girls must return to your tower. Mum and I have things to do."

I step forward. "No."

Mum blinks. "No?"

"This has gone on long enough," I declare. "I deserve some answers." I gesture across Huntress and Kaps. "We all do."

Mum and Da share a long look. Da is first to speak. "True."

My parents take off in a new direction. The area behind the courtroom is so complex, even an ant could lose its way. Eventually, we step into a black granite chamber that's lined with dark velvet benches.

Da takes a seat. "You wanted to talk."

"I do," I state. "But we must wait until everyone has arrived."

The door slams open. My Rhodes stands framed on the threshold. His green eyes flash. My heart soars.

"And now, we're all here." My rhana moves to stand at my side. "Any problems with my Rhodes joining us?"

"On the contrary," says Mum. "We approve of your union."

I tilt my head, trying to process this news. It's yet another bit of strangeness to add atop the growing pile of today's odd happenings.

"You approve," I repeat.

"Absolutely," states Da.

"Then why not make your consent formal?" asks Rhodes. "Why allow Killian a claim?"

"Right on," adds Kaps. "Killian should be in a dungeon, not in consideration for a seat at Thanksgiving."

I frown. "Thanksgiving?"

"Human thing," says Kaps.

Mum takes a seat beside Da. "Allow us to explain. Your father and I have been very busy these last three months, and there hasn't been time to fully brief you." She presses her fingertips between her brows. I know this move from Mum. She is deeply worried.

"Allow me, luv," says Tempest.

"Please."

"It comes down to this," says Da. "Chimera's soul is still alive."

"You are certain?" I ask.

"My vision was precise," answers Mum. "Chimera's spirit exists. And it inspires not only Killian, but also an army that's five hundred thousand strong."

Her words slowly sink in. Five hundred thousand warriors? That's enough to take over Furonium.

"How does he manage it?" asks Huntress. "The Thorntails aren't wealthy."

"Chimera left behind a massive treasure hoard," adds Da. "It's more than enough to pay for an army to be fed, clothed, and housed."

"So where are they?" asks Kaps.

"On Earth," says Da. "We don't know the precise location where the troops is hidden. Believe me, we've looked. Killian's using a bloody brilliant spell to conceal them all."

"I've tried every counter-casting I can think of," says Mum. "Nothing. I even called in help from your extended family. The wizards of Striga ... archangels ... elementals ... they've all come up empty."

"That's why you've been so busy," I say.

"And it's why you locked us up," adds Kaps. "You thought the army might hit Furonium while you were gone."

"We couldn't risk losing you," says Da.

My mind sorts through everything I've learned. Killian is hiding an army that's a half-million strong, only no one knows where it is. My parents have been searching for information, but have come up empty. They placed my sisters and me into a tower to keep us safe in case of invasion. All of which raises another question.

"What about me and my Rhodes?" Speaking of my rhana, he wraps his arm around my shoulder. It's a protective gesture and is most welcome.

"At first, we were shocked you had found your rhana so quickly," says Mum. "But we've adjusted to the idea. You two are clearly bonded. It would be cruel to keep you apart. That isn't why we've waited to give our approval."

"Then why?" asks Rhodes.

"Killian," replies Dad. "He could unleash his army tomorrow. There's no reason for him to wait. No *logical* reason."

A chill runs up my back. "There's only a romantic one. Me."

Rhodes nods slowly. "I hate to admit this, but there's some logic in Killian's plan as well. Everyone knows you've been with Killian for years."

I gasp. "As a prisoner."

"The truth isn't what matters here," says Huntress. "It's what Killian can spin to the people of Furonium. If his goal is to replace Chimera on the throne, then having you along gives legitimacy."

"We've wanted to give our approval," adds Mum. "But once that happens, we lose our only stalling tactic with Killian. He'll invade and fast."

Sadly, I can see my parents' logic on this one. "So we need Killian to reveal the location of his army."

"Wherever that force is hiding, you'll find Chimera's soul there as well," says Da. "You can bank on that."

"Killian kept Chimera's spirit in a box before," I state. "Do you think there's another container of some kind?"

Da smiles, but there's no cheer in it. "There's *always* been another container. The real one."

I frown. This line of discussion is going somewhere that I definitely don't want to visit. There must be another option. "What about the other realms? Can't they send troops to Furonium?"

Mum sighs. "If we bulk up our forces, then Killian will attack right away."

Huntress nods. "It's what I'd do."

"We have one advantage," says Mum. "Right now, Killian is distracted. We need to keep him that way. Your father and I have agents following Killian all the time. At some point,

Killian will make a mistake. Then we'll find both the army and Chimera.

"My father's spirit is what gives Killian his strength and intellect," adds Da. "Once we truly erase Chimera, then Killian won't have the guts to brew his own *cuppa tea*, as the saying goes."

I lean my head on my Rhodes' shoulder. This is all so much. My parents approve of my Rhodes. Chimera's spirit is still alive. And Killian has a hidden army ready to take over our realm. It all adds up to one fact.

"You need me to distract Killian," I state. "That way, he'll reveal the location of both Chimera and the Triumvirate army."

"We've thought this through a thousand times," says Mum. "That's the only tactic with a chance of working."

"You can't make Zin fight a half million warriors," says Kaps.

"No one has to fight anyone," counters Rhodes. "We only need to go to Earth and knock Killian off his game."

"Precisely," agrees Ma. "All we need are a few more clues. Then the Kathikon will find Chimera. Once we destroy that evil dragon's spirit once and for all, then Killian and the rest will crumple."

The many facts spin about my head in a haze. In the end, four simple words become clear. "Chimera is the key," I state.

"That's right," says Mum.

I look to where Rhodes' palm curls around my shoulder. Part of me wants to grab his hand and run. The thought fills my soul with joy. After ll, Rhodes and I could do anything. Be anywhere. Plus, I now know my family approves of my rhana.

Yet the truth holds me in place. I'm the only thing stopping Killian, Chimera, and their army.

Da heads for the exit. "It's your decision, little luv. The Triumvirate army could attack at any time. If you're going to Earth as a distraction, then we need to know now." Da opens the door. "You'll want to discuss this alone. Come along, everyone."

All my family files out of the room, leaving behind me, Rhodes ... and the largest problem I've ever faced.

RHODES

*O*nce we're alone, I angle my body toward Zin. "Let me get this straight. You'd actually consider returning to Earth?"

"I would."

My chest swells with pride. "My strong rhana."

Zin's eyes sparkle with light and life. "And when we go in, there's only one cover that will work."

I nod. "The band."

A knock sounds on the door. Empress Portia's voice echoes into the room. "Are you ready?"

"We are," I state.

Zin's family files back into the room. Once everyone is settled, Zin and I explain our plan: taking Cool Daze on tour.

"Killian couldn't stand it when Zin was with us before," I explain. "He kept turning up along the route, that kind of thing. You want him distracted? A Cool Daze tour will do it."

"This is great!" exclaims Kaps. "Plus, the rest of the band

members will totally be into it. You two have a hit single! They've been whining to me daily about a tour."

"What about the risk?" asks Zin.

I think through our band members. "Bash and Livingston will be fine," I reply. "They're both patriots. If it helps keep Furonium safe, then they'll do it. Chase might be different. I'll talk to him. If he says *no*, then it isn't the end of the world. It's not like we don't need another guitar player anyway."

"Oh!" Kaps claps. "And there's Abracadawn. We could start touring at any time."

"What is this Abraca… thing?" asks Da.

"It's a huge tour that's already in place," answers Kaps. "Whenever we want a spot on stage, we'll have it."

"So the children have a plan ready to go." Mum turns to Da. "It's a great cover."

My father nods. "We won't be far, either. We'll keep you under constant surveillance as well."

Kaps raises her hand. "Huntress and I will be on the bus, too."

Zin nods. "Killian will reveal the location of Chimera and his army. And this time, we shall fully destroy my evil grandfather."

I grin. That's my fierce and beautiful rhana, all right.

ZINNIA

THE NEXT DAY

*T*his is odd.

In some ways, it feels as if the last three months haven't happened. I stand in front of Nikki's metal wagon at a random highway stop in Forest Park, Illinois. There is a burger establishment, some devices for providing gasoline, and a stand-alone telephone. We've been to many places like this before.

The people appear the same as well. There is the drumming-man, Bash. He is a young and bald fellow with chocolate-colored skin. Beside him stands the lanky Livingston, who wears a cow mask today.

I'd forgotten how that man wore masks everywhere.

Kaps strides across the lot, her duffle bag slung across her shoulders. She marches past me without a word. All the while, Kaps' gaze stays locked on her data pad. It is a wonder how she walks and reads from that device at the same time.

Huntress follows behind her, no doubt watching my sister's every step.

Nearby, Rhodes hauls equipment into the bottom of the bus. Once the last container is in place, my rhana steps over to my side. "Strange, isn't it?"

"I was thinking the same thing."

Now Chase You Dick saunters across the lot. He has spikey brown hair, a baby face, and a twisted bandanna around his head that serves as a sweatband.

I've figured out that Chase You Dick is not his true name. It is only Chase. Yet Chase You Dick does sum up more of his personality. For instance, right now Chase You Dick is trying to set a variety of odd items into the bottom of the bus. Nikki is not pleased and wishes him to cease this activity. Chase will not stop.

He really is Chase You Dick.

Nikki is a good human who takes care of us. She's like our tough grandma in a sari who keeps everything moving. We should respect her wishes when it comes to the metal wagon. That is why Rhodes and I step closer.

"Thank goodness you two are here." Nikki hitches her thumb toward Chase. "Will the pair of you talk some sense into this nut?"

I focus on Chase You Dick. "What are you doing to Nikki?" I ask.

"I'm just bringing along some essentials."

Nikki sets her fist on her hip. "You're packing skis, six tennis rackets, and a dozen baseball bats into my bus. Why is this necessary? Have you changed from music to running sports teams?"

Chase You Dick rolls his eyes. "I've got to keep training,

Nikki. And I'm tough on my equipment. You wouldn't understand."

"Oh, I understand all right," says Nikki. "Put this stuff—" she gestures across the pile of stuff "—under your mattress. Not in my trunk."

"But my skis won't fit," whines Chase.

Now it is Nikki's turn to rolls her eyes. "Boo. Hoo."

Rhodes nods. "Nikki's right. Under the bunk or it stays home."

"Since when do you run things?" asks Chase You Dick.

"Since always, Chase." Rhodes lowers his voice. "Move the junk or move your ass home. Your pick."

I must admit, I find it rather enjoyable when Rhodes becomes growly. Especially when the object of his frustration is Chase You Dick.

With lots of grumbling, Chase You Dick separates some items from others. I scan them all carefully. Chase You Dick mentioned these were for his training. Yet there is only one kind of training these items could be for. Battle. The bat makes sense, but the other two items appear rather useless.

Nikki steps closer, breaking up my thoughts. "Thanks for helping out with Chase."

"Any time," says Rhodes.

Nikki frowns. "If I'd known you were heading to Arizona, I wouldn't be parked outside Chicago right now. You can take a plane to Mesa, you know."

I tilt my head. "But we are only a few days away. Driving with you is more enjoyable."

Rhodes nods. "What Zin said."

At this point, Livingston steps up. After moving the look-ing-holes on his cow mask, Livingston views us from his right eye. "Guess what, Nikki? I can light my farts on fire. Wanna see?"

Nikki doesn't answer Livingston. Instead, she turns to me and Rhodes once more. "Then again, it is probably best to trust me for your travel. This band is an airport incident waiting to happen." She taps her chin, thinking. "I'll try to take back roads as well."

"Thanks," says Rhodes. "The bus doesn't say Cool Daze on it either, so that's all good."

Next Rhodes and I step into the vehicle proper. Nothing here has changed. There are forward-facing seats up front. In the middle, a set of small tables line either side of the vehicle. And in the back, there are two rows of bunk beds. We have more time on this journey, so we can stay in a hotel one night. But the bunk beds ensure we can make tight dates if necessary.

I quickly find my old bunk. It is occupied by a metal box filled with all sorts of interesting tools. Nikki steps up behind me.

"Sorry, I left this here."

"Not to worry," I state. "These items are amazing. Look at this wire." An idea hits me. "I could use these implements to make you some weapons."

Nikki winks. "You can do that any time. I'd love to see what you come up with." She removes her box of tools and I slip onto my bunk. The moment I close my small curtains, something amazing happens.

A white light begins to blink on my wrist cuff.

14

RHODES

I toss my bag onto the bunk below Zin's. A bit of window sits above my mattress. Someone taped up pictures of Cool Daze. Not that I don't like seeing images of my own face. But it's already a strange day. I don't need to add to the overall oddness. I tear down the pics.

That's when I see her.

Sienna stands outside bus.

Above my bunk, Zin opens her curtains. "My Rhodes," she whispers.

"I see her."

Zin and I have already discussed how Sienna told me she'd never speak to me again. Having my mother visit me here on Earth is a shocker, to say the least.

"What do you wish to do?" asks Zin.

"I'll go to her."

"And do you wish company?"

"Nah, I got it."

"All right. I shall wait here and think good things about you."

Leaning into the bunk, I kiss her nose. "Thanks."

I turn toward the front of the bus and pause. What will my mother want? Which Sienna will I meet this time? Straightening my shoulders, I stride outside.

Sienna stands a few yards away. She wears a loose and colorful dress. Some folks from the diner point at her. I can almost hear their voices through the window. *Is that THE Sienna?*

I march closer. "Hey, Sienna."

"Hello."

A long and awkward pause follows. At last, Sienna breaks the silence. "This is a good bus. Sturdy. Clean."

"Yeah. Our driver runs a tight ship."

Sienna reaches into pocket and pulls out a small metal pin of a cello. "I had these made for my first world tour. Afterwards, I always brought one on the road with me. For luck." She hands it over.

I take the small pin from her palm. "Thanks."

For the first time, I notice Atlas standing closer to the diner itself. He's in sweats and hoodie with the cowl down. *Smart move.* Not that humans would see his greenish skin, but they might sense something is off. I nod in his direction.

Sienna sighs. "Your uncle and I had better get going."

"Sure thing."

Yet neither of us move. There's so much to say, but I don't know where to start. Sienna opens her mouth, and for a moment, I think she may launch into a speech about undying love. She wags her winger at me. "Don't lose my pin."

I chuckle. I wouldn't trade Sienna for all the so-called normal mothers in the world. "I won't."

Sienna steps off toward the diner. Atlas meets her half way. Then he does something I never expected.

Atlas sets his arm around Sienna's shoulder.

This is my mother, who can barely tolerate a three-second hug from her own son. And yet this a good thirty seconds of shoulder contact going on here. My eyes widen. Are they getting together? It's been years since Titan died, so it's all fair game. And I want them both to be happy.

Still. What a day.

Shaking my head, I speed back onto the bus. I must help Zin kill the ghost of an evil dragon emperor. Time to set aside thoughts of my mother's love life. I can deal with that later.

Or, on second thought, *never.*

15

ZINNIA

*M*y Rhodes re-enters the bus. Soon he stands by my bunk. He appears both happy and confused.

"How did it go?" I ask.

"Sienna gave me a pin." He holds up a small metal cello. "With my mother, that's like throwing me a goodbye party. It's all good."

"I am fine as well." I twist my silver bracelet on my wrist.

It is time, Zinnia. Bring your rhana in on your secret.

I take in a long breath. "I need to make a call."

"Private?"

"Yes."

"There's a pay phone across the lot."

I lift my chin. "I would like you to come with me."

My Rhodes rewards me with a dazzling smile. "Sure."

We leave the metal wagon to find a small phone on a heavy metal stick. It is odd, but functional. I dial the number. Someone picks up after the first ring.

"Jade here."

"It is me. Zinnia." I am no expert at phone etiquette, but this seems like a reasonable way to start a conversation. "My bracelet lit up."

"I've got news for you. Your Gracie has a sister. Her name is Faith."

Excitement zings through my body. "Is she alive?"

"Abso-freaking-lutely. And she's with the Triumvirate."

All this time, my Rhodes waits nearby. He stares off at the main road, seemingly watching the cars stream by. That mean he's close if I need him, but not hanging on every word. I really do have the best rhana.

"How many…" I close my eyes, trying to remember the name. "How many of the third estate are with her?"

"Not many."

I frown. "But I thought they supported the second estate. The warriors. There are a half million of them."

"That's the thing," says Jade. "I don't think they're alive."

"The warriors are dead?"

"Or just not human. Whatever they are, they don't need much in the way of care and maintenance. That's all I've got so far. I'll be in touch if I find out anything else."

"Thank you, Jade."

After hanging up, I turn to my Rhodes. His brows are all scrunched together. "Is that Jade?" He asks. "As in Jade Brooch?"

"It is," I reply. "Huntress introduced us." I scan all around. There's no one close enough to overhear. If my plan will work, I must tell Rhodes. Plus, it's not just a matter of my guilty conscience nagging at me. Gracie has a sister! I must gather all the help I can find. And my Rhodes is the best.

"There was a woman who helped me," I explain.

"Back when you were in the desert?"

"That's night. I loved her deeply. Her name is Gracie and she's part of the Triumvirate. Or was. Gracie is dead now."

My Rhodes green eyes fill with sympathy. "That's rough, Zin. No wonder you needed time to sort things out. Who did it?"

"Killian."

"That bastard." Muscles flex along my Rhodes' neck. "Yet another reason he deserves to be in a dungeon."

Now, I could go on for years about my hatred of Killian, but there are more important topics at this point. "There is good news as well. Jade just told me that Gracie has a sister. Faith. She's still with the Triumvirate."

My Rhodes' features turn unreadable. "She may like it there, Zin."

"I know. But Gracie saved me. If there's anything I can do for Faith…" I leave the logic out there, mostly because I cannot force myself to say anything more.

"Still my fierce warrior." My Rhodes exhales. "So we keep an eye out for Faith. And did I hear something about warriors?"

"Jade says they aren't alive. They might not be dead, either. Just not human."

"That is some weird crap."

"This is true." I look to the metal wagon. "The others must be brought up to speed."

My Rhodes nods. "We've got a two-day drive to Arizona. Plenty of time to chat."

Which is a comforting thought indeed.

16

ZINNIA

After the call, my Rhodes and I step up into the metal wagon once more. Once we reach the top step, Nikki waves me over.

"Yes, Nikki?" I ask.

"This is your show, right?" She gestures between me and Rhodes. "The two of you?"

I nod. "We have the hit single."

"Then why don't you say a little something to the troops?" Nikki hands me a small black box. "You can give us a send off."

I gingerly clasp the item in my hands. It is cold and odd. Nikki points to the right-hand side. "There's a button there. You depress it to talk to the bus."

"All right." I look to Rhodes. "What do you think?"

"Good idea," says my rhana. "You want to go first?"

I love gadgets of all kinds, mostly because I never saw any before. I'd say I want to hand over this talking box, but that would be a lie. I depress the button on the right-hand side. "Hello?"

My voice echoes through the metal wagon. I beam. *It works.*

I continue. "Nikki has asked me and my Rhodes to speak a few words before we leave on tour. I should like to thank you for joining us. We are scheduled to play a concert in Arizona and then murder the ghost of Emperor Chimera. Technically my parent's private guard are tasked with killing him, but I would prefer to do the job myself."

A lot of silence follows.

Like a gopher, Livingston pops his head up over his seat. "I am not killing anything."

"We know this," I continue.

My Rhodes gestures to the speaking box. "May I?"

"Sure."

My Rhodes takes over. "We all talked about this. Nikki, Bash, Livingston, and Chase … none of you are expected to do anything but go on tour. But the rest of us are on a secret mission. Emphasis on *secret.* There's a reason we're all in an unmarked bus with Nikki to keep us in line. No one goes blabbing about Cool Daze and what we're up to. When you're off the bus, you look and act like a regular person. Our show at Abracadawn is an audience surprise. Let's keep it that way."

"Works for me," says Bash. He is rapidly becoming my favorite band member. Outside of my Rhodes, of course.

I take back the talking box. "So there you have it. Stay out of our way and you'll probably live."

Once again, silence is the only reply.

Nikki retakes her device and sets it on a small holder. I lean in close. "How did I do?" I ask.

"That was great," says Nikki. "I'm sure everyone is excited not to die."

"Good," I grin.

We peel out of the parking lot and start our adventure.

17

RHODES

HOURS LATER

6 AM.

Zin and I spent most of the night chatting with Huntress and Kaps. We told them all about what we've learned on how the Triumvirate army is not alive. After that, we came up with a lot of crazy theories. Kaps shared that the second estate must be after dragon artifacts. Although that theory looked a little thin, it wasn't like we had anything better to replace it with. The sky was brightening by the time Zin and I get to sleep.

Which brings us to the present moment.

Zin and I are now sandwiched into the same bunk, trying to get some rest. Too bad Kaps stands in the outside aisle, flashing us images from her data pad.

Okay, it's mostly me she's talking to.

"What do you think of this one?" asks Kaps. At least, Zin is gently snoring.

I don't even bother to look. "I love it."

Kaps turns the data pad back to face herself once again. "I take it back. This is garbage. Nothing but a packet of old dragon scales. Hardly an artifact worth recovering." She scans a few more screens. "Oh! Maybe this?" She flips the data pad toward me once more.

Now, I spent years being Kaps' personal monkey boy. The job description involved putting up with her crap and working with Huntress to keep her alive. It was about as fun as it sounds, but I did it out of loyalty to my rhana. Now Zinnia is back. Turns out, putting up with Kaps is a hard habit to break.

I yawn. "Love that one, too."

Kaps turns the data pad back toward her face and frowns. "Oh, no. This is a replica dragon tail cuff from the thirteenth century. Who cares about that?"

"No one."

"Oh, oh, oh! I've got it. This is the super mega prize, my friend. Not one, but *two* Wurtzite daggers. These are incredibly rare and can cut through anything. I'm talking diamonds, dragon scales, souls, the works. And it isn't too far away from here."

"Kaps, it's not my job to chat about this stuff with you."

"It never was, really. And still you don't stop."

Zin smacks her lips, looks up and smiles. She mouths one word. *Morning.*

I kiss her on the top of her head. My rhana is precious.

Zin angles her gaze toward the window. Growing up in a cave means things like highways are fascinating for her. Together, we cuddle and watch the traffic. Meanwhile, Kaps keeps droning on about Wurtzite daggers.

A supply van for Abracadawn drives by. It's a modern style vehicle with a shiny steel exterior. As the van speeds past, I see a woman reflected on the surface. And not a picture of a woman, either. This is a real person who blinks, breathes, and wears a long brown cloak. Unfortunately, her features are unreadable. Is this woman happy, sad, or enraged? It's impossible to tell. The image vanishes.

"Did you see that?" I ask Zin.

"Yes. That woman looked like …" she swallows. "Gracie."

That news spins about my head for a moment. It stops at a single conclusion. "Do you think that was Faith?"

"I know it was. Faith must be using some kind of magic to contact me. But why? There is nothing I can do for her right now."

"Maybe Faith just wants you to know she's ready for you."

"I suppose. Still, it is hard to wait. I wish things did not go so slowly."

"I understand that." *And I do.* There aren't many people —*either shifters or humans*—who would handle this situation as well as my Zin. "Is there anything I can do?"

"Not now. I need some time alone. And I have a project to keep my mind off things."

"Okay. I'll be in the bunk below if you need anything."

Slipping out of the bunk, I find Kaps is gone. She's moved over to the table area, where Kaps now talk Wurtzite daggers with Huntress. I take the opportunity to slide into the lower bunk.

And I fall asleep.

ZINNIA

*H*ours pass as I focus on my project. It uses supplies from Nikki's tool box and is soothing in the extreme. Why? Gracie used to bring me wire like Nikki's. I would add barbs or wind it into a whip. Weapons creation was an important part of my learning. Doing it again comforts me with memories of my lost friend. My project is finally complete when I hear Nikki's voice on the speaker.

"We're stopping for burgers!"

I do not need to hear this announcement twice. Leaving my new weapon behind, I slip out of my bunk. My Rhodes is awake and sitting up on his mattress. His sweet face is all creased with marks from his pillow.

"Did you sleep well?" I ask.

"Yeah. How about you? Feeling better?"

"Better and hungry. Let us feast on burgers."

My Rhodes shoots me a sly look. "Anything else?"

"And chocolate, certainly."

We leave the bus.

19

RHODES

*Z*in and I are half-way across the parking lot when Chase rushes up behind us.

"What the hell?" calls Chase. "Who messed with my tennis racket?" As evidence, he holds said racket in his right hand. The netting shines with a particularly metallic sheen.

Clearly, Zin was a busy girl while I was napping.

Zinnia pauses and beams. "It is a suitable weapon now."

Chase stomps his foot. "You can't go around ruining other people's stuff. It's for tennis balls." He raises a sample ball in his left hand.

"And now it functions better." Zinnia grabs the racket and ball. For his part, Chase is too stunned to stop her. Zin tosses the ball into the air, brings racket down and *whoosh*. That tennis ball gets shredded. Zin hands the racket back to Chase. "You're welcome."

Chase stands in the parking lot, staring between his killer tennis racket and new pile of shredded gunk. I'd feel bad for the guy, but he ruined two speakers and three guitars so far this year. Having one of his tennis rackets get *improved* is nothing in comparison.

But it does give me an idea.

If Zin and I are going to be stuck on the road anyway, we might as well make some memories.

20

ZINNIA

*A*fter stepping into the diner, I speed right to the counter. No tables for me, thank you. At the counter, there's no extra wait for burgers.

A girl must have priorities.

Many of mine involve burgers.

My Rhodes steps into the diner behind me. He stops by Nikki's table. They chat for a few minutes and there are many glances in my direction. Perhaps Nikki wishes to relocate to the counter where she can access burgers more quickly as well. Our bus driver and I share a passion for meat sandwiches.

Eventually my Rhodes leaves Nikki to sit on a little round stool next to mine. I already know my rhana's order, so there are three cheeseburgers coming his way. We enjoy our meal.

For my part, I eat four burgers.

Sadly, the meal is not pleasant for Bash and Chase You Dick. It seems our drummer took offense to something Chase You Dick said about Bash's mother. They've almost gotten into a fight two or three times today, and we haven't even been on the bus that long. Bash storms out of the diner. At least, our drummer enjoyed his burger.

Back on the bus, Rhodes and I slip back onto our bunks. We're only a few miles away from the diner when Nikki gets on her small speaker. "Great news! We've a nice motel for tonight. But I'll drop off Rhodes and Zinnia first."

I slide half-way off my mattress so I hang upside-down before Rhode's bunk. Then I pull apart the curtains. "What have you planned?" I ask.

He blinks innocently at me. The man really has lethal eyelashes. "Planned?"

All the blood is pooling in my head, so I can't remain in this position forever. "You are a sneaky man."

"Always." Rhodes winks.

I hoist myself back into my bunk and wait.

Whatever is coming, it will be good.

21

RHODES

I do have a rather awesome plan for this evening. To make it happen, I had to bribe Chase, but that was easily done. Now all that remains is a short wait.

To kill some time, Zin and I hang at the bus' tables, playing blackjack with Huntress and Kaps. As Zin's request, we're playing for Hershey's Kisses instead of money. Works for me. Zin enjoys the aspect of hiding her cards, so she holds them right against her nose while looking suspiciously across the table.

It's adorable.

Kaps only half-pays attention. All her focus is on her data pad and those two Wurtzite daggers. After a while, I can't keep my mouth shut.

"Hey, Kaps."

Her gaze stays glued to the data pad. "What?"

"Want a hit?" It's my turn as dealer.

"Huh?"

Zin keeps her cards by her nose. "My Rhodes is asking if you wish another card, my sister."

Huntress and I exchange a dry look. Kaps knows how to play blackjack.

"No, not, uh, needed."

I level her a serious look. "Kaps."

At last, she looks up from her data pad. "What?" She's all innocent eyes and a serious case of bedhead. "I got locations on both Wurtzite daggers. They're in different locations, but neither are far away. I think I'll go after the first blade."

Zin lowers her cards. This is getting serious. "You are leaving us? But we must find Chimera and—" she lowers her voice "K-I-L-L him."

Livingston pops his head over the back of the next row of seats. "I am not killing some dead emperor." He wears a pig mask today.

"We got that already," I say.

Livingston slowly lowers back into his seat, but the way he does it? The motion looks like he's a piggy sinking into a mud puddle.

Kaps waves her hand. "I won't leave right now."

"Right now?" repeats Zin. *She's a smart one, my rhana.* Took me years to catch that little verbal asterisk in Kaps' promises.

Kaps turns to me. "You know my system, right?"

I've only heard this one a thousand times. "No emotions. No entanglements."

Kaps grins. "Exactly. That's how—when I go after any dragon artifact—I can be sure there are no problems afterward."

Now Huntress gets into the act. "Does that mean there's no price on your head anymore?"

Zin scans Kaps, then turns to me. I keep forgetting how my rhana lived in a cave for years, followed by a few months in a tower with her sisters.

"What is on her head?" asks Zin.

"Nothing physical," I explain. "The saying means that L'Griffe is unhappy with your sister and her habit of stealing—"

"Liberating," injects Kaps.

I give Kaps the side-eye. "Of taking things that the L'Griffe already want. We'll leave it at that. L'Griffe has placed a bounty on Kaps. Anyone who brings her to them gets gold."

Kaps lifts her chin. "I consider it a mark of professional respect."

"L'Griffe is Furor mafia," says Huntress. "You're royalty. There is nothing professional or parallel between you."

Zin's eyes widen. "I learned about the mafia. There are certain battle tactics to use against them." She focuses on Kaps. "You are not a trained warrior, my sister. Do not steal from them."

Kaps tosses her cards down. "I'm not a thief. These are Furor artifacts that belong back in our homeland."

Chase saunters up to the table. "Are you out of the game, Kaps? Can I take your place?"

Huntress, Zinnia, and I all speak in unison. "No."

Kaps climbs over the tabletop to leave her corner seat by the window. She crushes a few Hershey's Kisses along the way. Once she's back in the main aisle, Kaps turns to Chase. "How about showing me your sports collection?"

"I sold it to Rhodes," says Chase.

"You did?" asks Kaps.

Zin turns to me. "He did?"

I wink in Zin's direction. "I am a man of many interests."

Chase is undeterred. He's been trying to hook up with Kaps for years. One thing I'll say for Zin's sister, though. She sticks to her motto.

No emotions. No entanglements.

Chase doesn't stand a chance. He snaps his fingers. "I've got it. I just glued new stuff to my guitar. Want to see?"

I shake my head. Chase better not have screwed up the instrument's sound. Otherwise, that will make another busted guitar to add to his list.

"Why, I would love to see what you've done to your guitar," answers Kaps. "It should be a very accepting conversation where no one gangs up on me."

"Right," says Chase. "And maybe afterwards, we can make out."

This time, Kaps, Huntress, Zin and I all speak at once. "No."

And we mean it.

ZINNIA

We play blackjack at the table; I consume most of the chocolate kisses. The sun barely touches the horizon as Nikki stops the metal wagon. I glance out the window. We're supposed to be staying in a motel tonight. This place is no hotel, though.

Instead, it's a small building with a large white sign that reads, Midlands Tennis.

Instantly, my Rhodes' plan comes into focus. "We are to play tennis together?"

"Yeah." He grins. "And not with rackets that slice things up."

I crumple my face in confusion. "Those aren't weapons?"

"No," explains Huntress. "You use the rackets to hit the ball back and forth. It's a game."

This still seems strange. "Do you try to smash the ball into someone's face?"

Rhodes chuckles. "Come on. I'll show you." He picks up a bag from under the opposite table.

"Be careful with my stuff," says Chase.

"It's mine now," counters my Rhodes.

We stride to the front of the metal wagon. Nikki heaves a lever that opens the front door. "You know where the motel is, right? Should be a short walk away for you. Or flight. Whatever."

"I've got it," says my Rhodes.

"Thank you, Nikki." I wave goodbye as we step off.

The metal wagon roars away. My Rhodes and I stand before a small building. Beyond the tiny structure, there are series of rectangular shapes beaten onto the ground, reminding me of patterns on a blanket.

I step up to the building's window. It is boarded over. Deserted. The rectangular grounds are all surrounded by chain link fences. Those entry doors are locked up with heavy chains.

"It's closed. Is this regular for such a place?" I ask.

"It's out of business," explains my Rhodes. "I didn't want us to be bothered with humans." His gaze catches mine. Lines of fire and attraction burn between us.

I straighten my cropped T-shirt and shorts. "Is this what one wears to play tennis?"

"You look great." For his part, my rhana sports low-slung jeans and a white T.

My Rhodes winks. Emerald light flares up behind him. A moment later, great green wings appear behind his back. "Ready?" he asks.

"Sure."

My Rhodes spreads his wings. With a few pumps, he soars over the locked fence to land on the other side. The odd-shaped bag stays gripped in his fist. "Now you."

The order is a little bossy, yet for some reason that only makes me wish to kiss him. Closing my eyes, I summon my own dragon shifter energy. My wings appear and in short order, I stand beside my Rhodes.

"Ready for your lesson?" he asks.

"In the game of tennis."

"That's right." He gestures around. "This is called a court."

"As in for a king, but with small green balls."

My Rhodes chuckles. "Something like that." Kneeling down, my Rhodes unzips the bag. He pulls out a racket. I can't help but notice that it isn't the racket I fixed up as a weapon.

"Now we need some tennis balls." Curling his free fist by his shoulder, my Rhodes closes his eyes. A sense of magic and excitement fills the air. Tiny bolts of lighting circle my rhana's arm. I step closer, my mouth open in awe. I'd never seen my Rhodes use his Electrophus powers like this before.

My Rhodes moves his arm so it's parallel with the ground. The lightning bolts arc off his hand to the nearby courts and greenery. The electric cords then curl back to my Rhodes. Only when they return, the bolts now carry tennis balls with them. Dozens and dozens. They all fall across the court and bounce about. My Rhodes lowers his hand. The spell is over.

Leaning down, my Rhodes picks up a nearby tennis ball. "Not bad," he says. "A little singed, but usable."

"How did you know they were nearby?"

"It's the nature of courts. Tennis balls get everywhere. Now, I'll show you how to serve." My Rhodes picks up a nearby ball and tosses it into the air. Then he leaps up and slams the ball across the court. It's a ballet of movement and strength. "If you were on the other side, you'd hit the ball back."

Walking over to the bag, I pull out another racket and scoop a ball from the ground. Standing up, I focus my inner energy, just as I do before a battle. After tossing the ball in the air, I whack at it with my own racket.

The sphere slams into the court and keeps going down. A moment later, there's a small hole in the ground with smoke curling up from it.

I bite my lips together. "Oops?"

"You've got a mean serve," says my Rhodes. "Just need to streamline your energy. May I show you?"

"Sure."

After setting aside his own racket, my Rhodes steps up behind me. Delicious pressure erupts along my back and legs as my Rhodes curls his body behind mine. His body radiates heat. My Rhodes slides his fingertips along my arms. He sets a tennis ball into my left hand. His right hand grabs my wrist. He leans in until his voice is low and rumbling in my ear.

"First toss the ball up gently. You've got that part down. We need to work on your swing." My Rhodes guides my right hand and racket in a series of arcs. "Nice and easy. Got it?"

"Yes." My voice comes out rather husky.

"Now, let's give it a try."

With my Rhodes behind me, I toss the ball into the air. Using the motion he showed, I strike the racket against the ball. It speeds across the court to bounce around on the other side. I turn around to face my rhana.

"See?" he asks. "You did it."

"Yes." I grip the bottom of his T-shirt and pull it upwards to expose his stomach. "Yes?"

My Rhodes nods. Gripping the bottom of his shirt, he pulls it off and tosses it aside. In the moonlight, the planes of muscle on his chest seem more defined. "There's no one around for miles, Zin."

"Good."

Gripping my shirt, I pull my top off as well. My Rhodes reaches forward. With the gentlest of touches, he brushes his fingers along the curve of my bra. My insides go on fire. Sure, my Rhodes and I have been alone-ish on the bus. Still, it isn't easy to get sexy when your sisters and a pack of strangers are nearby. And Kaps is forever popping in to show new pictures on her data pad.

But here? No one around for miles.

My Rhodes pulls down the cups of my bra, and kisses my breasts in turn. That's a rocket of sensation, right there. He looks up at me and grins. "Are you enjoying your lesson?"

"Yes. So. Much."

My Rhodes sets his mouth onto my nipple again and I groan. I run my hands across his head. His military brush cut feels as amazing as I'd imagined.

That's when it happens.

A shadow passes over the moon.

My Rhodes releases my nipple from his mouth and pulls up the cups of my bra. "I'm afraid the rest of our lesson must get cut short," he says.

My head has trouble processing this news. "But there's no one around for miles."

"That's not true anymore." He picks up my T and hands it over. "That shadow? Your parents just flew by." He pulls his own T-shirt on. "They'll be here any minute."

"Oh." In this moment, I can't imagine any news I want less.

RHODES

*Z*in still seems in a haze, so I help guide her top back on. For my part, I make certain to untuck my own T. Luckily it's a loose one, so it hides how attracted I am to Zinnia.

Damn, I thought this was the perfect plan to get alone time with my rhana … only I forgot that Tempest and Portia promised to be close by.

Ah well. There will be time for me and Zin. Just not this very second.

Two dragons swoop down from the night skies. It's hard to see their forms beyond the fact that both are massive. At the last moment, the pair transform into human shape with great wings. They land on the tennis court before us. The wings vanish. It's Tempest and Portia, Emperor and Empress of Furonium.

"Mum! Da!" Zin rushes over to give them both big hugs. Does the thought occur to me that I had their daughter half-naked two minutes ago?

Hard to forget.

Tempest fixes me with a serious stare. The guy is a greater demon of lust. No question about one fact. He knows exactly what Zin and I were up to.

"What have you learned?" asks Tempest.

Well, he's not threatening to punch my face in, so I guess we're good here.

"Not that you can learn much on a bus," adds Portia quickly. "But Tempest thought you may have news." Unlike Tempest, Portia seems oblivious.

"There is news," I reply. "The Triumvirate army is not alive."

"Not living." Tempest taps his chin. "Perhaps it's an army of the undead. Interesting."

"That would explain why we haven't found any signs of their operation," adds Portia. "A force that large would need food, tents, and medicine … all on a huge scale. We've run across nothing. But a magical army of some kind? That would be easier to hide."

Tempest nods. "I focused too much on Chimera's missing treasure hoard. We assumed it was being used to hire mercenaries."

"There's more," adds Zin. "While we were on the highway, a silver bus passed us by. I saw a Triumvirate reflected on the exterior."

"Mirrors are magical gateways," says Portia. "It's something to look into."

"Any word from the Kathikon?" asks Zin. "Am I successful distraction?"

"Yes," answers Portia. "They say he is acting rather erratically. We are confident he'll make a mistake and soon." She glances around the court. "What were you two doing here?"

"Tennis," says Zin. She does a good job of answering smoothly.

"Tennis," repeats Portia. "But your rackets are on the ground." Her eyes narrow.

Tempest wraps his arm around Portia's waist. "We're all staying at the same motel tonight. Shall we fly there together?"

So that's what we do. It may be short in terms of time, but the silence along the way is deafening. Once we reach the motel, I walk Zin to her room. After the door swings open, I grip the top threshold. That stops me from pulling Zin into my arms. I scan the outer walkway. No one else is around.

"We good?" I ask.

"With my parents, you mean?"

I nod.

"They're adjusting. I mean, they're lust demons, so this shouldn't be a shock."

"True." I lean in closer to Zin. She closes the space between us. We share the hottest, longest kiss of my life. I break it off because if I don't, I don't know where this will go. And Zin's parents are somewhere nearby.

"See you back on the bus," I say.

Zin winks and slowly closes the door.

That girl. I've never wanted anyone more in my life.

ZINNIA

*T*he next morning, we all enter the metal wagon early. This includes me, Rhodes, Kaps, Huntress, Livingston, Bash, and Chase You Dick. There's no sign of my parents, but they're certainly nearby. Most likely, the pair are flying around in dragon form somewhere beyond the clouds.

I take my regular seat the blackjack table along with Huntress, Kaps, and my Rhodes. Today, Kaps does not look at her data pad at all. I consider this more alarming than when she was obsessed with it.

Nikki places the metal wagon into gear. She picks up the small talking box. "Today's the day. We hit the Abracadawn after lunch."

The vehicle rolls out. As we close in on the concert site, the chatter on the metal wagon dies down. More cars stream past us, many painted with the words Abracadawn along the sides.

At last, we reach our destination. It's a small city surrounded by a desert of scrubby grass and dried earth. The place is set up like three beads on a string. The first area is a fair that's complete with carnival rides and food trucks. Second comes the concert grounds. And third is the workers' camp. That's where we'll be staying.

"See that?" asks my Rhodes. He points to a far off fence.

"It's made from shiny metal, just like the van." A fresh sight catches my interest. "And that thing is formed from even more metal."

I point to a spot between the fair grounds and concert area: a silver spire. Closing my eyes, I try to sense the electric zing of magic against my skin. Nothing.

I shake my head. "All those mirrors. There should be a magical signature in the air. Do you catch anything?"

"Not a bit."

I shrug. "Perhaps this is just a human concert after all."

Still, I cannot shake the sense that magic is at work here. And it has nothing to do with humans.

ZINNIA

*M*inutes later, my Rhodes and I march through a maze of red tents. Kaps and Huntress follow closely behind. All around us, workers speed along the winding paths about the structures. Some humans carry tools; others tote foodstuffs.

My Rhodes and I pause before a smallish tent in the back corner of the lot. Number 19. That's the girl's dwelling for Abracadawn.

My Rhodes pulls up the entrance flap, looks inside, and lets the fabric fall again. "Looks clean and set up. I'll be back once I settle the guys in." He adjusts my sunglasses and floppy hat. Outside the bus, we need to keep a low profile.

I wink. "See you when I see you." Those guys are a handful.

My Rhodes chuckles and steps away.

Hoisting my duffle onto my shoulders, I step inside our tent. Huntress and Kaps follow. Inside, it's a simple set up. Three air mattresses line the floor. Some trunks and fabric folding chairs lay about. A mini-fridge hums away in one corner.

Huntress and I set our bags onto nearby trunks. Kaps leaves her pack on.

I gesture toward Kaps' bag. "Rehearsal starts in a few hours."

"About that," says Kaps. "I might not make it."

I frown. "Why?"

"The Wurtzite dagger I want—it's only a few days away. And more importantly, it's basically unguarded. I'll be back before you know it."

"But not in time for the concert," I state.

"Come on." Kaps' eyes glimmer with excitement. "Wurtzite dagger. Think about it. What are the chances you'll find Chimera in the next few days? Pretty slim, right? And when you do face him, a Wurtzite dagger would be a big bonus."

"You said there was a second dagger," says Huntress. "It is supposed to be closer to this spot."

Kaps shrugs. "My sources say it's too well guarded."

"Sources?" asks Huntress.

"Fine," answers Kaps. "Jade Brooch says it's too well guarded. The second dagger is just with some random human. It will be easy peasy. And the guy's in Vegas. Think about it. A drunk guy running around with one of our sacred relics. Can you see how simple that would be to recover?"

I spin this news through my mind. "You know what? I think you're right."

Kaps folds her arms over her chest. "Of course, I am."

Huntress tilts her head. "And you're certain that dagger can cut through anything?"

Kaps shoots us a thumbs-up. "Diamonds. Dragon scales.

Un-killable ghosts. This is the ticket."

A long pause follows. Moving as one, we all share a hug. I just found my sisters. The thought of losing Kaps tears at my heart.

"Be safe," I say.

Kaps fairly skips out of the tent. After she's gone, Huntress and I share a long look. Huntress is the one who breaks the silence.

"Rehearsal starts in a few hours," she states. "What's your plan?"

I pull a notebook from my bag. Its pages are filled with lyrics and sheet music. "I'll look over our set before rehearsal. You?"

Huntress glances to the exit flap. "I'll scope out the fair grounds. Perhaps there's something that may be useful."

"Good plan. And thanks, Huntress."

After Huntress is gone, I flop down onto my mattress and flip through my notebook. I've a photographic memory, though. As a result, this review isn't really helpful.

After a few minutes, the entrance flap to my tent rustles. My Rhodes peeps his head in. I beam.

"Want to go exploring?" he asks.

"Love to. What did you do with the guys?"

"I've decided they are big boys and can handle themselves." He tosses his duffel onto the ground. "I'm staying with the girls."

"Kaps took off so you'll have your own bed and everything."

"Fair enough."

I toss my notebook into my bag. "In that case, let's go explore."

RHODES

*Z*in and I stroll around the Abracadawn fair grounds. It's a warren of little streets that end with the silver spire. Some pathways are lined with food trucks. Others feature stalls of T-shirts or posters of different bands. There's also a Ferris Wheel, Tunnel of Love, and even one of those pirate ships that swings back and forth. I guess if you can't fly, this is a big deal.

Speaking of humans, none of them notice us. Both Zin and I keep our hats and sunglasses firmly in place. It helps that most humans wear costumes. Everything is here from cartoon characters, comic book villains, and even a few dragons. With so much coolness on display, no one cares about me and Zin.

We reach the spire itself and I have to be honest, it's a bit of a let-down. The thing is huge, steel, and reflective, but there's not a ride inside or anything. It's more of a landmark. On the other side of the spire are the concert grounds. The setup is a lot like our gig at Trance-A-Dance. Small square areas are set aside with mini-stages. Those are for warm-up and local acts. At the end, there's the main arena, which is where we'll play tomorrow night.

I'm about to suggest we go back and get some fried waffles when I notice her. The woman from the reflection in the van: a wiry and gray-haired lady in a brown hooded cloak. I pause and turn to Zin.

"Is that?" I ask.

"Yes, it's Faith."

The woman disappears into the crowd.

Zin and I follow.

ZINNIA

I can't believe it. Faith is here.

Gracie's sister.

My Rhodes and I push through the crowd. Along the way, my hat gets knocked off. Someone grabs my wrist.

It isn't my Rhodes.

Turning around, I see a human in a Cool Daze T-Shirt. "Aren't you Zin E. Ah?"

Someone else speaks up. "That's absolutely Zin E. Ah. You look just like the video."

My eyes widen. *That's right.* Someone took video and me and my Rhodes playing *Our Song*. A small group of humans forms around us.

"And you're Rhodes!" cries another guy.

Within seconds, the small gathering swells to a sizable mob. A hundred handhelds flash as they take pictures and video. More voices sound from the crowd.

"There was a schedule change for tomorrow night," says one.

"Are you playing?" asks another.

"Sing for us now," orders a third.

Someone grabs my dreads and that's it. I look to my Rhodes. "We need to get out of here."

He nods and glances toward the sky.

Good idea, that.

Now it is unfortunate that we have lost Faith in the crowd. However, I shall not wait around to get human-handled by strangers. Plus, I know exactly how my Rhodes wants to escape. As I said, it is a fine concept.

"On three," I state. "One, two, three."

At that count, both my Rhodes and I leap up while transforming into our dragon shapes. Stretching our wings, we take to the skies. From the human perspective, we simply disappeared. My Rhodes and I hover above the crowd for a moment. More voices echo toward us.

"Where did they go?"

"That's a viral moment."

"I bet they're playing tonight."

I grin and look to my Rhodes. "The humans don't suspect a thing."

"They never do." My rhana smiles, which is an extra-interesting look on his long green snout.

"Rehearsal begins in ten minutes. Shall we fly to the main stage?"

"Sure."

And even though it's a short flight to the main stage itself, I still scan the ground for any sign of a woman in a long brown cloak.

Yet I don't see Faith at all.

28

RHODES

Zin and I land at the back of the main concert space. It's a massive, open field surrounded by more tall metal panels. The stage looms on the far side of the ground. It's pretty standard stuff for a festival crowd: a big black platform that's framed by massive screens. Camera crews flank either side of the structure.

A pair of human guards approach me and Zin. Both wear Abracadawn jackets.

"How'd you get in here?" asks one.

"We're actually dragons who flew over all your security checks," I reply.

It's best to be totally honest with humans. Tell them about magic and they'll make up their own excuses as to why that's bull.

"Must be the new guy," says the second guard. "I bet these two just walked past him."

Case in point. Here, I'm totally honest with the human. *We're dragons, dude.* Still, he comes up with his own explanation. Works every time.

"We're with the band," I continue. "Do you need our IDs or something?"

The first guard's eyes widen. "Oh, wait. You're Zin E. Ah and Rhodes. Sure, go on ahead. The King of Abracadawn is waiting for you."

Zin frowns. "King?"

"The guy who runs Abracadawn," answers the second guard. "We just call him king. And I love your single." He thumps his fist against his chest. "Gets me every time."

"Thanks." Zin blushes.

Taking Zin's hand in mine, we start the long trek toward the main stage. Even from a distance, I can see that Bash and Livingston are already here. My brows lift with surprise. Chase is on time. He's talking to some guy in a suit; must be that so-called King of Abracadawn.

As we step closer, I can't believe the change in Chase. Usually he's angry, passed out, or whining. I've never seen the guy smile this much before. Who knew he had it in him?

We'd only gone a few yards when Zin freezes. Her hand trembles in my grasp. That's not like my rhana.

"What's wrong?" I ask.

"That guy." Zin nods toward the man in the suit.

"He's the King of Abracadawn," I state. "The guards talked about him before."

"No," says Zin. Now her voice takes on an edge of rage. "He's far more than that."

The man turns around.

Oh, damn.

It's Killian.

29

ZINNIA

*K*illian is here.

My jailer.

Kidnapper.

The man who murdered Gracie.

Every muscle in my body tightens with rage.

For his part, Killian opens his arms wide. "Rhodes! Zinnia! So good to see you!"

I do not open my arms. Instead, I glare at my nemesis. "You murdered Gracie."

"Ah, ah, ah." Killian wags his finger from side to side, as if I am nothing but a naughty child. "Your mother absolved me of any crimes. And now I run the most popular musical happening in the world."

I scan the concert space with a new appreciation. For months, someone had been luring Kaps into joining Abracadawn. Then we saw Faith reflected in the silver van. And here, the metal panels are omnipresent. Magic is at work.

If Killian is with Abracadawn, it's not from a love of music.

Could the Triumvirate army be here somehow? It might help explain why they're hard to find.

"What?" asks Killian. "No loving greeting from my betrothed?" He looks to Rhodes. "How about you? No big hello from a future corpse?"

My Rhodes' palm turns slick with sweat. Outside that, I can see no sign that Killian upsets him. "We're all future corpses, Killian. You especially."

"Naughty words." Killian winks. "Why don't you come up on stage and begin rehearsal?"

My Rhodes turns to me. Our gazes lock. All the determination in the after-realms shines in his green eyes. At this point, both of us would like to leave. We can't. Chimera and the Triumvirate army must be found.

We share a nod. *This is happening.*

Still hand in hand, my Rhodes and I step onto the stage itself. All the while, I think through my advice from Kaps.

B-A-D.

Breathe.

Activate.

Discharge.

If only I could breathe fire, I'd melt Killian's face. Even so, no matter how deeply I inhale, I hear no click in my chest. The fire won't come.

Once we're on stage, someone slaps a headset on me. Another person guides me to stand at the center. Meanwhile, my Rhodes goes to his guitar. Chase You Dick saunters over.

"Want to know a secret?" asks Chase You Dick.

"No." I pretend to be fascinated by fiddling with the microphone that arcs from my headset to my mouth.

"I've been working with Killian all along."

That gets my attention. "Liar."

"Killian didn't want to move in too early. He likes you for some reason."

Now, I would love to flatten Chase You Dick about ten different ways to sundown. But there are two good reasons not to do so. First, we need to find Chimera and the Triumvirate army. Fighting a member of my band does not move me closer to that goal. And second, Chase You Dick has no muscle tone and even slower reflexes. There is no sport in destroying one such as him.

I fix him with a serious gaze. "You'd better get in place. Rehearsal's starting."

Thankfully, Chase You Dick does as told.

Rehearsal begins.

30

RHODES

*T*he rehearsal is a rough one. It takes me a half-hour to chill out enough where I can strum my guitar without being in danger of pulling off the strings. My thoughts keep rolling back to a single topic.

Killian is the so-called King of Abracadawn.

That Thorntail killer has been working from behind the scenes to lure Zin here for months. Yet another reason to hate the guy.

Once I get my head into the gig, it becomes a challenge to connect to the other band members. Everyone goes at a different rhythm. It's the space and reverb that makes it hard to hear what's real and what's an echo.

Plus, it doesn't help that Bash keeps ignoring his drum cues so he can glare at Chase. It's no secret that Bash already hates Chase's guts. But the fact that Chase has been helping Killian? That only makes the rage burn hotter.

For his part, Livingston has a great time. He wears a fish

mask today. I have no idea how the guy sees out of the side-ways eye holes.

Kaps and Huntress are a no-show. Which is shocking and not, all at the same time. Kaps skipping rehearsal is no big surprise. In fact, it would be a bigger deal if she showed up. Huntress is another matter. I would have thought she'd stay close. Something must have happened. I set that thought aside for later.

Once I get in my headspace, I keep my focus on my music and Zin. She's new to both crowds and performing, yet my rhana handles herself like a pro. Eventually, we all get it together enough to nail our set. Happily, we're only performing a few Cool Daze tunes followed by *Our Song*.

At last, the rehearsal is over. We took all afternoon and now the sky darkens. Zin and I head backstage. Killian corners us there.

"Good job," he says.

"What do you want, Killian?" I ask.

"Just being friendly." Killian smiles, but the grin doesn't meet his eyes.

Zin stares him down. She's all badass calm, but once again, I feel her hand tremble in mine. We step away. Killian moves to block our path.

"Don't think about escaping or using magic," says Killian. "This whole place reflects my power."

We don't say another word, but Zin and I share a quick glance. It's there in Zin's eyes. Killian said the words.

Reflects my power.

Zin knows it, same as I do.

Killian just admitted that the metal panels are all part of a spell.

Nice work, dickhead.

31

ZINNIA

Once we're away from the stage, my Rhodes and I slip into the periphery of our workers' city. We find a secluded spot and pause.

"Killian spoke about power reflecting," I state.

"And he's talking about the metal panels," finishes my Rhodes.

I shake my head. "Normally, when I feel magic, there is a vibration in the air. This place still holds none of that. Do you sense anything?"

"Zero. And I agree. This many panels would be reflecting magic back and forth, creating a vortex of power. Even humans should be able to detect it."

I gesture to the silver spire. "And that should be giving out the most energy of all."

My Rhodes rubs his neck and thinks things through. "In theory, it could generate enough magic to hide an army."

A figure steps up from the nearby shadows. I heave in a shocked breath.

It's Faith.

RHODES

I blink.

Focus.

Blink some more.

No, that's really Faith.

And she stands only a few yards away.

Up close, I catch a better look at her. Faith got a lanky build, long gray hair, and a face that's etched deep with worry lines. She sets her finger across her lips in a universal motion for silence.

Zin and I nod.

Faith slips off into the night.

We follow.

With every step, more excitement churns through my nervous system. Ever since I saw Faith reflected in a silver van, I'd wondered what her story could be.

Finally, I can get some answers.

Faith moves closer to one of the panels. Up close, these

things tower twenty feet high. At the base of each, a number has been punched into the metal.

Faith pauses before panel 956.

For a moment, Faith's image is reflected in the shiny metal. Then she steps into her makeshift mirror and vanishes.

My brows lift. That's no regular panel. It's a magical portal.

For me and Zin, we have no question about what to do next. While still holding hands, we step through the mirror as well.

33

ZINNIA

*S*tepping though the metal panel is like falling into cold water. One moment, my body is warm and dry. The next, a thousand icy pins bite into my skin. Only instead of cold, the sense that tears into me is magic.

It takes a moment to adjust to the reality beyond panel 956. My mind soaks in every detail around me. The place is just like the world we just left, only deserted and covered in dust. The sky hangs at the moment right between night and morning.

Faith steps up to me and my Rhodes. "We can talk here, so long as we keep our voices low." She hands us a pair of brown robes. "Put these on. If anyone asks, you are water servants."

I slip on my robe and pull up the hood. My Rhodes does the same. The process takes forever, though. The arm holes seem to hide on me and the hood is held back with a series of snaps. It's infuriating. I want to get past placing on my disguise and start talking to Faith. There is so much I need to discover.

At last, I am as hidden as I'll ever be. I focus on our new friend.

"You're Faith, aren't you?" I ask. "Gracie's sister?"

"Yes." She smiles, a movement that makes all her frown lines light up with joy. There's so much of Gracie in that face. My heart soars.

Word fall from me in a tumble. "Gracie helped me. I want to do the same for you."

"Bless you, child." Faith takes my hands in hers. Her skin is cool and papery. "Gracie and I wanted the same thing: to be free."

My Rhodes eyes Faith from head to toe. "So why not leave?" There's a note in his voice which says, *why should we believe anything you have to say?*

And he's right. Gracie was the one who taught me battle strategy should be based on what I *observe*, not what I *wish*.

"You can't stay here long," says Faith. "The mirror tracks when strangers pass through without cloaks."

"Convenient," says my Rhodes.

"This is a reflected mini-realm. See that silver spire? It's a duplicate of the one on Earth. Only this version is packed with magic. Every silver panel reflects and enhances the energy. Do you sense the magic?"

This is such familiar and beloved ground. How many hours did I spend with Gracie while she told me facts and asked me questions?

"The magic is so powerful, it almost hurts," I state.

"That's right," says Faith. "And Chimera's soul resides within that silver spire."

"What's inside, exactly?" asks my Rhodes.

"I do not know," answers Faith. "I am not one of those who

serves in the spire. But I know those who do. They shall leave the spire door open for you tomorrow night at 11 PM."

"That's right after our concert ends," I say.

My Rhodes tilts his head. "So you know these people enough that they'll leave a door open for you ... but they won't tell you what's inside the silver spire?"

I grip my Rhodes' wrist. "Faith is risking a lot to help us."

Faith raises her hands, palms forward. "No, it is a fair question. Our ways here are strange. I wish there were time to explain them all. Yet I can do one thing before you go."

My Rhodes narrows his eyes. "What's that?"

Faith straightens her stance. "Show you the second estate."

My breath catches. *This is it.* The moment my parents have been working toward for months. It's the very secret we've all tried so hard to crack.

My Rhodes and I are about to see the Triumvirate army.

34

RHODES

*S*ee Chimera's secret army?
I'm game.

Faith steps off into the shadows. Zin and I follow her past deserted versions of the workers' camp. The tents all stand at the ready, just covered in dust and dripping cobwebs.

Speeding past the encampment, we soon reach the main concert stage. My blood runs cold.

There is certainly a performance stage here. Plus, it looks just like its earthly counterpart. There are monitors and equipment—everything appears just as we left it after rehearsal.

It's the audience that's different.

This place is packed with row after row of warriors. They stand slumped yet in formation, as if they'd fallen asleep on their feet. And all of them are made from dragon treasure. The Triumvirate fighters are a mishmash of silver coins, golden goblets, and shimmering jewels. My breath catches.

Chimera's lost dragon hoard.

This must be what happened to it.

The silver spire flares to life. A beam of white light erupts from its peak. A booming voice echoes all around us.

"Awaken!"

Beside me, Zinnia whispers a single word. "Chimera."

I'd been suspicious of Faith before. Hell, I'm still wary. But she did say that Chimera's soul resided in the spire. That part of her story checks out.

Over on the concert green, the warriors snap to attention. Thousands of jeweled eyes stare forward.

Faith turns to us, her features tight with worry. "You must go. Come back in tomorrow. Only you two and with these robes. 11 PM at the spire. That's all I can manage."

"Thank you," whispers Zin.

Together, my rhana and I speed back to our reality. All the while, a single thought rattles about my mind.

We need a plan.

35

ZINNIA

*O*nce we pass through mirror 956, my Rhodes and I speed back to our tent. Everything we learned keeps churning through my thoughts. I'm bursting to discuss it all with my rhana.

We enter the tent to find it is already occupied. Jade and Huntress await us. Both sit on folding chairs.

Jade eyes us from head to toe. "Faith found you, eh?"

I pull the robe off. Turns out, removing it is rather easy. "Yes, she did."

My Rhodes steps forward. "Let me guess. You're Jade Brooch."

"That I am," says Jade.

"We have lots of news," I announce.

"So do we," counters Huntress. "Mum and Da are on their way."

My parents stride through the entrance flap. It is odd to see them in human clothes. Da is dressed in jeans and a T-shirt. Mum sports a simple white sundress. Both wear anxious looks.

"Huntress, what's going on?" asks Mum.

A better question I couldn't have asked myself.

"Mum. Da. This is Jade Brooch. She's one of my best human contacts."

Jade bows her head. "A pleasure to meet you, your majesties."

"Good to meet anyone who helps my daughters," says Da.

"Jade uncovered some information," continues Huntress. "Kaps already left to seek a certain artifact—"

"Not again," sighs Mum.

"There's good news and bad news," continues Huntress. "The good news is that the item in question is a Wurtzite dagger. It can slice into anything: diamonds, dragon scales, and even spirits."

Da nods. "That would be helpful in killing Chimera, certainly."

"What's the bad news?" I ask.

"There's another party who's taken an interest in Kaps' mission," says Jade. "Your sister needs back-up."

Huntress rises. As always, she wears her battle leathers. "Jade and I off for Vegas to see how we can help. We leave immediately."

My Rhodes and I share a long look. We're thinking of the same thing. "That Wurtzite dagger might be more critical that we suspected, right?" I ask.

"Yes," replies my Rhodes. "The timing could be perfect."

"Timing for what?" asks Huntress.

"Jade connected us with a woman, Faith." I explain. "She just led us to Chimera's hidden compound."

My parents round on us. Every line of their bodies seems focused on one thought. *Tell us more.*

"The metal panels all around?" asks my Rhodes. "They're all part of a spell."

"I don't sense anything," says Mum.

"It's not one that works in this reality," I explain. "If you step through one of the metal panels, you enter a reflected mini-realm. It looks just like this one, only it's deserted and dusty. In that reality, Chimera's spirit exists inside the silver spire at the center of *that* version of this area."

"And we saw his army," adds my Rhodes. "It's Chimera's treasure hoard enchanted into the form of soldiers."

"Not human," whispers Mum.

"When can we go there?" asks Da.

"My Rhodes and I can slip back in tomorrow after our concert, but it is only a reconnaissance mission."

"Now I see," says Mum. "By the time Huntress returns with this weapon, you'll know where Chimera's spirit is held. Then we can use the Wurtzite dagger to kill him."

"That is the idea," I confirm.

Da folds his arms over his chest. "We should go in with you."

"Faith was specific," says my Rhodes. "Only me and Zinnia. 11 PM. The silver spire in the reflected mini-realm will be open. We'll get in, find out what's up with Chimera, and hightail it back."

Mum rests her hand on Da's forearm. "It's an information mission only. The children will be back quickly. And we can have all our dragons ready by the entrance."

"All the metal panels are marked," I add. "The one to the reflected mini-realm is number 956."

Da huffs out a breath. "Recon only, right?"

"Right," I confirm.

Mum scans the tent. "Your father and I should stay here. Add to your security."

"About that," I wince. "This event is run by Killian."

Da pales. "What?"

"He announced that to us today at rehearsal," says my Rhodes.

"In that case, we'll need to stay hidden," says Da. "If Killian sees us wandering about, he may suspect what we've discovered about Chimera and the reflected mini-realm. We've all worked too hard to bugger it up now."

"Agreed." Mum sweeps over to fold me in a big hug. We all say our goodbyes. Soon, it's just me and my Rhodes in the tent once more.

I focus on him. "We forgot one thing in our plan."

"What?"

"Killian. Once we leave the concert, he may follow us around again, just like he did today after rehearsal. We don't have a lot of time to try and lose him."

A slow smile rounds my Rhodes mouth. "I've an idea how we can fix that. Bash."

"I don't know him very well. Are you sure he can help?"

"Positive. I just need to zip over and have a quick chat with the guy. Be here when I get back?"

"Absolutely," I reply.

Once my Rhodes is gone, I scan the empty tent. A realization dawns. Huntress and Kaps are both gone now. My parents vowed to stay far away.

Tonight, my Rhodes and I will be alone in this tent.

36

RHODES

*I*t's takes a little doing, but I eventually find Bash on the tour bus. Turns out, he couldn't stand sharing the same tent with Livingston and Chase.

Can't blame the guy.

Our drummer sits at one of the tables mid-bus, flipping through the pages of the specialty program for tomorrow's concert. Zin and I are on the cover.

Bash wags the magazine-style program in his hands. "Did you see this? They're contraband until 11PM tomorrow night. There's a whole section on you two."

"Nah. I try to avoid that stuff. Anything on you?"

"I've got my own page in back. Makes me a happy drummer." He folds the program and sets it onto the tabletop. "What's up?"

I slide onto the seat across from him. "I've got a tricky situation here."

Bash rolls his eyes. "Are you about to tell me this is dangerous stuff again? Because I told you, being in a band with Kaps is already risky. I'd rather take chances for Zinnia any day."

"Thanks, but this is about something else. After Zin and I do *Our Song*, I need you to keep the audience going for a while. Zin and I must have a few minutes to escape. No Killian around, if you get my meaning."

"We've only got three songs. You and Zin play in all of them. We can't keep the audience distracted with music."

"I know. I have another idea."

Turns out, Bash loves the concept.

37

RHODES

*B*ash and I gab for a little bit. Mostly, we sync up about some things for tomorrow night's gig. Zin and I had to run off right after rehearsal, so we never got a chance to go through notes. And to be honest, Bash is the only one who counts. If our drummer has it down, then he'll keep the other band members in line.

It's close to midnight when I return to our tent. Zin sits atop her mattress, reading a book. She wears a long T-shirt and a smile.

"Everything go well with Bash?"

"We're all set. You want to hear details?"

"No." Zin rises, steps over to the tent entrance, and clicks a lock over the zipper. No one can get in or out.

I scan the tent. Empty. It's just me and Zin. In all the excitement, I forgot that both Kaps and Huntress are gone tonight. It's tempting to think that Zin may want to pick up where we left off at the tennis court. Then again, my rhana has spent most of her life locked away from the world. It's taking her a while to adjust to foods that aren't burgers. I figure sex is way off the menu.

Zin turns to me and pulls off her nightshirt. She's naked underneath. *Damn.* Every inch of this woman is beyond gorgeous.

My body instantly heats. "I'd ask if you're certain about this, but…"

"I definitely am."

Zin steps up, wraps her arms around my neck, and pulls me into a kiss. It's one of the hottest things that's ever happened to me. While stripping off my clothes, I walk us backward to the bed. We lay down side by side and nose to nose.

"Is this your first time?"

"Yes. Kaps told me everything."

"And what did she say?"

"We're lust demons. Sex doesn't hurt, even during first sex. And we don't get pregnant unless we both want to."

I run my fingertip down the curve of her jawline. "Those are the highlights, yes." *Sometimes, it's good to be a demon.*

"And something else."

"Hmm?"

"I'm a warrior. We do nothing without a plan of attack."

I like where this is going. "Do your worst, Zin."

So she does.

ZINNIA

itching my leg over my Rhodes' knee, I quickly flip him over. Now my rhana is on his back. I sit astride him with my knees braced by his hips. My hands press his wrists against the mattress. A bead of sweat rolls down the line of hair that trails his belly. I've never seen anything more beautiful.

"I have ideas," I say.

My Rhodes gives me a sly half-smile. "And I like them."

"Good."

Little by little, I lower my hips and take my Rhodes inside me. We're now one person. Connected. Every nerve ending my body flares with heat. It's almost too much sensation. I heave in quick breaths.

My Rhodes slides his hands to my hips. "Breathe slowly, my rhana." His voice is low, soothing, and sexy, all at once.

I force out a long exhale. My body relaxes a bit.

"That's it." My Rhodes grips my hips more tightly. "This is

our rhana bond at work. It makes everything more intense."
He gently rocks beneath me. "Let me guide you."

The motion of his hips makes fresh heat curl within me.
"Yes, my rhana."

And so my Rhodes moves. Kisses. Touches. Adores. It is
one moment. It is forever. Hours pass before we find each
other on the other side of desire.

And I fall asleep in his arms.

ZINNIA

*W*hat a day.

My Rhodes and I spend much of the next day sleeping, kissing, and discussing how to best employ the Wurtzite dagger. After all, Kaps, Jade, and Huntress are all after the thing. No doubt, the weapon will be in our possession soon.

As the concert nears, my Rhodes and I get ready. We opt to wear jeans and T-Shirts. No fancy costumes, thank you very much. After the show, we'll be sneaking about a reflected mini-realm. Best to dress comfortably.

The few times we do leave the tent, Killian is always there. His eyes have always reminded me of a shark. Today his dark gaze flares with both hunger and triumph. It's a good thing my Rhodes gave our cloaks to Bash last night. Our drummer shall hide the items in a predetermined place where we can grab it after the show. If we tried to conceal them today, Killian would have noticed for certain.

When it's time for us to go backstage, a group of guards

accompany us. It's a short walk from our tent to the concert itself. Still, the journey reminds me of my childhood in the palace. At Firelord funerals, my family would all wear our royal best and step off to the Temple. Kathikon guards in ceremonial dress always marched along at our sides.

Which brings me to the present moment. I stand backstage, hidden in the wings. My Rhodes and the band wait nearby. A pool of shadows surround us. The darkness ends with a line of searing light on the main stage proper. It's a barrier between me—*the real Zin*—and Zin E. Ah, this person I've only begun to understand.

Killian stands at center stage with a microphone gripped in his fist. The fact this is a concert doesn't seem to change his choice of outfit. Killian wears his regular gray suit.

"Who's loving Abracadawn?" asks Killian.

The crowd roars.

"Who's ready to dance until the sun comes up?"

Another cheer follows.

"Abracadawn is pleased to announce our secret surprise act. The rumors are true! You're about to witness the first performance of *Our Song* since the tune went viral."

If I thought the cries were loud before, now the audience turns downright deafening. Excitement zings through my limbs. After all, these people are cheering for something me and my Rhodes created. Yet there is also an edge to the sound —something both hungry and angry. It reminds me of the shark look from Killian's eyes.

Focus, Zinnia. You're about to perform.

"Right here, on this stage, Abracadawn presents Cool Daze!"

Those words are followed by another searing cheer. Lights

pulse across the stage, blinding me. I remember our marks from rehearsal.

Twenty paces forward and pause.

As I march on stage, another cry rises up from the audience. Under the flashing lights, I spy the many bodies pressing toward us and being repulsed back by security. It's a kind of human wave that crashes upon the shore of our stage.

My Rhodes sets his hands on my shoulders. With gentle movements, he positions me more to center stage. Guess my calculations were a little off. My Rhodes kisses me once, gently. The crowd loves this.

Spinning about, I face the band. Everyone is in place. Raising my fist, I pump out a rhythm.

1, 2, 3...

Bash picks up the beat and we launch into our first tune.

Me and my crew
We dance, dance, dance
Guys eye me up
Don't stand a chance, chance, chance

The world fades away. I sing. The audience responds. Energy and life arcs between us.

Zin E. Ah is here.

My Rhodes comes up for the last number of the set. We play *Our Song.*

Gray or green or brown or yellow
Your look could change just like the rainbow
I wouldn't care
It's what we share

You're mine

Thousands of glow sticks pop to life in the surging sea of a crowd. Their energy may be raw—and more than a little frightening—yet it is real. And it comes from *Our Song*.

The performance ends. Voices raise in yet another cheer. I shoot my Rhodes the side-eye. He's been rather cagey about how we are to escape this place without Killian following us. My Rhodes says the perfect distraction will now follow.

Time to find out what that is.

RHODES

hat happens next is a thing of beauty. Bash gets up from his drum set and marches over to Chase. The cameras follow our drummer's every movement on the huge monitors surrounding the stage. The cameras zoom in as Bash pauses before Chase. The crowd goes silent. There's no mistaking the sense of drama. Audiences thrive on that kind of energy.

Then it happens.

Bash sucker punches Chase.

The pair get into a fight, or as much of one as you can get into when one guy—*meaning Bash*—is twice as big and mean as the other. Sure enough, Killian rushes out from side stage to break everything up.

It's our moment.

Zin and I are off to panel 956.

ZINNIA

*M*y Rhodes and I speed through the back stage. Bash left our robes by the back door, so we slip on our disguises and step outside. From there, it's a short walk to panel 956.

Soon My Rhodes and I step into the reflected mini-realm. This time the press of magic isn't as overwhelming. There's still no missing it, though.

Once we're on the other side, the place appears unchanged from yesterday. A gray sky hangs overhead. The Abracadawn fair grounds stretch out before us. All is deserted, dusty, and quiet.

This time, my Rhodes and I need no guide. We rush through the workers' area and pause before the main concert grounds. Unfortunately, we're already late on time. The fastest route to the silver spire is past the Triumvirate army.

We slip past the stage. Strange to think that only a few minutes ago, I stood on a mirrored version of this same spot, only it was free of cobwebs and fronted by an ocean of fans.

Now the audience are row after row of metal warriors, all of them with their shoulders slumped and heads bowed.

Perfect silence wraps about the scene. My heartbeat, footsteps, and even my breaths … everything sounds overly loud to my own ear. The metal soldiers do not stir.

My Rhodes and I reach the silver spire. Up close, it is more of an octagon than a rounded cone. Each of the eight panels are covered in a thin layer of dust. Like frost on a window, the tiny particles form odd shapes on the smooth metal.

My Rhodes points to a bottom panel. Sure enough, there's a break in the gleaming metal. It's a door.

And it's open.

We steal up to the door. So far, everything has gone to plan. I can't shake the feeling that's it's all too easy. Then again, losing Gracie wasn't simple. And finding Faith was an effort. Perhaps this is my past love of Gracie reaching into my present.

I can only hope.

My Rhodes silently pulls the door open. A slice of light cuts into the darkened interior. We step inside to find there is a small platform by the door. Beyond that, empty space yawns before us. We shuffle inside and look down into darkness.

The door closes behind us with the softest of clicks.

I grip the handle. Locked.

An electric sense of alarm moves through my nervous system. Something moves in the darkness. A thin beam of light shines out before us. It's as tall as I am.

That's when I realize it.

I look upon the slitted pupil of a reptile. As my vision adjusts to the dim light, I see that the eye is part of a massive dragon's head which sits atop a long neck. Like the Triumvirate army, the thing is formed completely from bits of treasure hoard.

The great head moves out of the shadows. Turns out, it's not alone. A total of three massive dragon heads look upon the tiny figures of me and my Rhodes as we stand on our thin ledge.

That's right. Chimera is a three-headed dragon.

My heart kicks so hard, I can feel my pulse throbbing at my throat.

"Welcome," say the trio of heads in unison. "Why don't you come in for a visit?"

The far right head slams into the stretch of spire wall above us. The entire structure shakes, rocking the thin ledge that we stand upon.

My Rhodes and I tumble off into darkness.

RHODES

*Z*in and I fall for for what feels like ages. The air smells of dried blood and dust.

Smack!

Both of us fall onto a moving pile of metal. I feel around me, trying to determine where we've landed.

Coins.

This must be more of Chimera's dragon hoard. Far below the reflective mini-realm, Chimera is living in a deep cave that's lit by torches. And it's filled with treasure of all kinds. Coins, diamonds, pearls, crowns, paintings … anything a dragon would value is piled high in this cavern.

And in the center of it all is a massive dragon made of silver, gold, and gemstones. Its three heads are focused on me and Zin.

"Behold my treasure hoard," say the heads in unison.

Stepping to Zin's side, I wrap my arm around her waist. We share a long look. Zin mouths two words. *Right time.*

I nod. *Agreed.*

Zin and I talked about what we'd do if Chimera discovered us. In the end, we decided our best chance would be to transform into our dragon selves, but to do so strategically. *We must find the right moment.* If we can surprise Chimera and attack, we may have a chance to end this. Or at the very least, escape with our lives.

At this point, one thing is certain. Chimera's three heads keep glaring at me and Zin. This isn't what you'd call a great moment for surprise attack. We simply must wait and hope something better arises.

A gentle glow shines from within the treasure-filled version of Chimera. A realization appears. The brightness must be his spirit. The great dragon lumbers over to a pile of ornate boxes. Once again, the heads speak in unison.

"Remember this, granddaughter? Before you, there stands a pile of soul boxes, just like the one you saw me in before."

Chimera opens his mouths. Smoke billows from his jaws to enter one of the boxes. That container lights up. From there, the smoke moves from box to box. Each one lights up as his spirit passes through.

"I remember," says Zin. "Your soul was supposedly stored in a box like those."

"As if some tiny container could be enough to keep me." Chimera brings up his front leg. *Crunch!* Bringing his front limb down, Chimera crushes the pile of soul boxes. "Do you understand now?"

Zin nods. "You were never in the soul box that I saw. Your spirit was housed here. What I saw was only a conduit from this horde to wherever I was waiting." If Zin is shocked to be chatting up her evil grandfather, she doesn't show it.

"Good," say the heads again. "You always were the smartest

of my my offspring. I only used the boxes to watch over your development. Oh, and to murder Killian's father. Isn't that right, slave?"

Killian steps forth from the shadows. Now that's no surprise. It isn't even shocking that Chase lurks behind him, looking exceptionally cocky.

"It is true, my master," says Killian.

"Are you surprised that Killian betrayed you?" asks Chimera.

Zin and I answer in unison. "No."

"What about this?" asks Chimera.

Faith steps forward. Zin stiffens beside me. My rhana puts on a brave face. Even so, this must be killing Zin inside.

Anger boils my blood. My claws extend, ready to hurt Faith for causing my rhana pain. It takes some focus, but I force my talons to retract. Now is not the time.

We must wait for our moment.

The first dragon head peels off. Arcing on its long neck, the creature focuses on Faith. "There used to be many of you, weren't there? Human warriors and servants. All are gone now. What happened?"

Faith swallows. "You killed them after the princess escaped."

Zin gasps. I don't blame her. It's not my rhana's fault that Chimera went on a murderous rampage. And Zin had no way of knowing it would happen. Still, it must wound her.

The first head keeps addressing Faith. "And what did you tell my granddaughter about today's little meeting?"

"That the servants opened a door to let her in," says Faith. The woman's manner is unreadable. Is she angry? Excited? It's impossible to tell.

"It was a lie, wasn't it?" asks Chimera.

"Yes, my master."

"And why would you do that?"

"To please you, my master."

The first head swoops back to look at me and Zin. "It does please me to take life. There is scant little to do while I await my rise to power once more."

Killian steps forward. "If you'd come to the surface, you'd see the reflected mini-realm above. It is a first of its kind in terms of magic. There is much to see."

The light within the Chimera flares more brightly. "This is my cave. Here is where I remain until I've taken on a living body again. You asked me to leave before, didn't you?"

Killian hangs his head. "Yes, my master."

"Come see the princess, you said. Display your mighty self to Furonium while taking Zinnia over, both body and soul."

My rage turns so intense, it's hard to pull in enough air. How can Chimera speak so coldly of his own flesh and blood?

Stay calm, Rhodes. Not yet.

"And what if I'd done such a thing?" asks Chimera. "I'd truly be dead now. So I'll stay here. I've waited long enough to rise again. A little longer won't hurt. And you can always bring me fresh entertainment." The third head swoops over stare at Chase, then clicks its teeth together.

"Tell it to leave me alone!" cries Chase.

The third head frowns. "How boring. I hate it when they whine."

All heads arc back to stare at me and Zin. "You'll provide a far more interesting end. Ladies first."

Moving forward, I place my body between Zin and the dragon made from treasure.

Not yet.

"I was going to kill her myself," says Chimera. "Now I think it would be more poetic for someone else to destroy my granddaughter." The first head peels off to address Faith once more. "You brought a weapon?"

Faith takes out a small blade from the folds of her cloak. Based on the angle, Chimera can't see what she holds. Zin and I can, though. It takes an effort, but I hide my surprise. I've seen pictures of this weapon before on Kaps' data pad. It's a Wurtzite dagger.

"Go on, my servant," orders Chimera. "Stab her."

Faith grips the dagger so the blade points down. "As you command."

My body almost vibrates with warrior energy. This has to be the moment. I can not stand by while someone injures my rhana. Turning, I meet Zin's gaze and whisper a single word.

"Now."

"No," whispers Zin. "Do nothing, Rhodes."

"You can't ask that."

"I can. I request this as your rhana. Trust me."

Anger and despair churn through me in equal measure. I want to grab Zin, transform into my dragon form, and fly far away from here.

Yet she is my rhana. I trust her.

I nod. "Go on."

ZINNIA

*G*o on.

Those two words from my Rhodes echo through my soul. He trusts me. But do I believe in myself?

Faith steps closer. Her footsteps crunch on the coins and jewelry under her feet.

As she gets nearer, there's no denying the truth. Faith looks so much like her sister.

Ah, my Gracie.

Memories flood my mind: Gracie reading romance stories as a treat for a good week of learning … How she'd always say, *fight the battle within before going abroad* … And the way her broken body lay on the ground after Killian sent demons after her. My heart both warms and breaks with the remembrances.

Faith isn't Gracie. I know this. Yet, Faith hides that Wurtzite blade from Chimera's view. The old dragon wouldn't have allowed a servant to carry the one weapon that could injure him.

Faith is trying to help me, I know it.

She steps closer. "My master commands your death."

"Chimera doesn't control you," I whisper. "He gives you strength and drives you with anger. But you are still your own master."

Chimera chuckles. "Slit her throat, Faith."

"Yes, my master." Faith pauses before me, raises her dagger, and sets the cool blade against my throat.

I tremble. This is crazy. What makes me think a mere human won't follow the orders of a three-headed ghost dragon made from treasure?

It doesn't make sense. Even so, I won't give up.

"You won't harm me," I state.

Faith presses the dagger against my skin. The edge nips my flesh. A thin rivulet of blood oozes down my throat.

"You're right," says Faith. "I won't."

She hands me the dagger. I quickly slip it into the sleeve of my robes.

Chimera howls with rage. Faith gasps. Looking down, I see the steely end of Chimera's tail has punched through Faith's chest.

"Worthless human," snarls Chimera. He pulls the tail loose. Faith tumbles forward. I fold her into my arms.

"No, this can't happen." I moan. "Not again."

Faith gives me a sad smile. "It's all right. I am free."

She closes her eyes. *Faith is gone.*

Leaning my head back, I let out my own howl of rage and despair.

44

RHODES

My poor Zin. She sits on a pile of gold, holding someone she values more than all the treasure in this hoard.

Faith is dead.

I kneel at Zin's side. "Come away," I whisper. "We need to be ready." I guide her back to standing.

"Useless servant," snarls Chimera. "Suppose I'll have to do it myself."

Killian steps forward once more. "You promised Zinnia to me."

Chimera sniffs. "I have another granddaughter. Take the weaker girl. She'll bear you plenty of dragonlings."

Killian stomps his foot. It sets off a small cascade of coins down a small fissure in the ground. For the first time, I notice the uneven nature of the cave floor. Lots of breaks and pits. Not something for a dragon to worry about, but certainly a factor to keep in mind while in human form.

"I want Zinnia!" snaps Killian.

"You desire what you're given," counters Chimera.

The lines of Killian's face pull tight with rage. "Yes, master."

The three heads swirl back to focus on me and Zin. Once again, they speak in unison. "The question is, what is the best way to kill? Bite, stab, or crush?"

This must be the moment. I look to Zin. Determination shines in her eyes.

"Not yet," she whispers. "But soon."

45

ZINNIA

Things are not looking good for me and my Rhodes. However, it is Chase You Dick who throws up his hands.

"I didn't sign up for this," whines Chase You Dick. "No one said anything about dragon attacks. I wanted to see someone stab Zin, sure. But not this."

I do a double take. Chase You Dick showed up here to watch me get killed. Talk about dumb ideas. Yet knowing our guitar player, I am not surprised.

"Quiet," snarls Killian.

"No, get me out of here." Chase You Dick rounds on Killian. "Where's the door out of this place? Where's the—"

One of Chimera's heads swoops down to grab our guitar player in his jaws. In one swift bite, Chase You Dick is cut in half. His two sides tumble onto separate piles of gold.

My Rhodes looks to me. "Lightning."

I slip the edge of the Wurtzite dagger out of my sleeve. "Climbing."

We share a nod.

Only two words were spoken, yet our plan is clear. My Rhodes will stay in human form while he releases lightning at Chimera. Meanwhile, I'll try to attack the beast from another angle. With a Wurtzite dagger in my possession, I have a better chance of wielding it in my human shape.

In other words, if we can better fight as humans, there is no need to change into dragon form.

My Rhodes spreads his arms wide. An intricate web of lightning instantly appears across his arms and torso. Keeping his arms straight, my Rhodes claps his hands together before him. A heavy bolt of lightning twists off my Rhodes' fingers and slams right into Chimera.

For a moment, the strike loosens the make-up of Chimera's treasure-body. A handful of coins tumble to the ground. It doesn't last long, though. Chimera's body quickly regains its form. He lumbers toward my Rhodes.

Time for me to move.

While Chimera is focused on my Rhodes, I race around behind the dragon, ready to scale up his tail. Once I reach Chimera's chest, I can go after his heart or throats with my new dagger. Preferably all of the above.

I get one foot on Chimera's tail when someone grabs me from behind.

Killian.

"You are my bride," he hisses. "Accept it."

I allow the Wurtzite dagger to slide to my hand. *Enough is enough.* Lifting my arm, I stab Killian right through the heart. "Consider our engagement broken."

Killian slumps backward, dead. He tumbles onto the ground. After that, he keeps going.

Oh, no.

I'd noticed before that the floor is pockmarked with pits and fissures. Killian can't be falling into one of those; the guy has my Wurtzite dagger embedded in his chest. I need it to fight Chimera.

I leap after Killian, only I'm not fast enough. His body slips into a darkened pit. It takes all my skill not to tumble in after him. Balancing at the edge of the fall, I pinwheel my arms and regain my footing.

Somewhere far below, Killian's body lands with a thud.

This is not good. Yet what did Gracie always say? *If one plan fails, try another.*

A fresh idea appears.

I rush toward Chimera, ready to scale up his back once more.

This simply must work.

It's time for dragons.

RHODES

*I*f you really want trouble, shoot a massive bolt of lightning into the chest of a three-headed, enchanted ghost of a dragon with an impermeable treasure-body.

Chimera rushes me, his three heads snapping. I saw what one of those things did to Chase. The guy didn't stand a chance.

Pulling my fists against my chest, I transform my lighting into a shield. Sure enough, the heads strike at me, one after another. Each lunge crashes into my shield. The force knocks me on my ass. I alter my shield into an arced shape that I can protect myself under.

Smash! Smash! Smash!

Chimera's heads slam into my shield, over and over. My lightning holds, but with each strike my shield gets less curved. At this rate, I'll be crushed to death and soon.

Through the web of lightning, I see a figure standing on Chimera's shoulders.

It's Zin.

And she's smiling.

"Now!" she cries.

Zin leaps up into the air while transforming into her beautiful black and crimson dragon. She swoops down, picking up a pile of metal chests in her talons. She drops them on Chimera's heads.

That gets his attention. Chimera's great necks arc as he seeks out his new enemy.

This is the moment. *At last.* I transform into my own dragon form and take to the air beside Zinnia. Opening my jaws, I let out a fresh stream of lightning, more powerful than anything I've ever released before.

Take that, old man.

ZINNIA

My Rhodes and I spin and dive about Chimera's three heads. My grandfather is larger than we are. But bigger also means slower. My Rhodes and I are more nimble. We fly about in an intricate dance that keeps Chimera occupied.

It won't kill him, though.

Every so often, my Rhodes sets loose another blast of lighting. Just as before, the bolts impact Chimera's body. Treasure falls from the strike point, but causes no lasting damage.

We need more fire power. Literally.

Kaps' advice runs through my head.

Breathe.

Activate.

Discharge.

I inhale over and over. Nothing happens. My Rhodes switches things up by diving into the ground, as if the gold coins were one of the oceans his kind master so easily.

Chimera snaps at the air above the point where my Rhodes disappeared.

A moment later, my Rhodes bursts up from another part of the cavern. It's a clever move, but there is no mistaking the fact that my Rhodes is moving ever more slowly.

We can't keep doing this forever.

I suck in more breaths. *Come on, chest!* I need that clicking noise. Fire must strike.

That's when it happens. Chimera's second head snaps his jaws around my Rhodes' dragon belly. His blade teeth haven't broken through my rhana's skin, but that won't last for long.

Panic streams through my limbs. This isn't happening.

Chimera caught my Rhodes.

It's over. I can't do this.

The first head swoops toward me. I hover a safe distance away. "Come closer, granddaughter. Cause me no more trouble and I'll allow you both to live."

My Rhodes arcs his neck toward me. The familiar lines of his eel-like face focus on me. "Fry him, Zin."

The words send a charge of confidence and love through my system.

Click, click, click.

The firestarter in my chest bursts to life. Flames grow within me.

Breathe.

Activate.

Discharge.

Opening my jaws, I exhale a stream of flame right into Chimera's face. Some gold coins melt. The metal drips off his face, reminding me of so many tears.

"What?" asks Chimera. "You can't breathe fire."

I let out another blast, this one hot enough to make Chimera step back. The dragon's second head loses its grip on my Rhodes. My rhana flies free.

Yes.

Together, my Rhodes and I circle Chimera. While I send out volley after volley of flame, my Rhodes does the same with lightning. At first, Chimera's heads snap at us, trying to fight back.

Then, Chimera tries to run.

His treasure-body melts away as he attempts to escape. With every lumbering step, Chimera gets smaller and smaller. More plates, gems, and rings drip from his form. Soon there's nothing left of Chimera but a small container that's decorated with a three headed dragon.

Huh. Turns out, the old dragon's spirit was stored in a soul box all the time, just one that was wrapped in the body of a jeweled giant. Everything was faked-up to look like more, just like Chimera himself.

My Rhodes and I send one more volley right at the soul box.

It explodes.

RHODES

B OOM!

For such a small container, it lets out an ear-splitting explosion. Zin circles the spot.

"Is he gone?" she asks.

"One way to know for certain." I glance up toward the exit and reflected mini-realm beyond.

"Right," says Zin. "The soldiers. If they're still around, we've got more trouble."

Zin and I angle our bodies upward. Pumping our wings, we quickly reach the spire that sits atop Chimera's cave.

I look to Zin. "Want to make our own exit?"

"Yes, my rhana."

As we fly upward, Zin blasts the metal spire with her flames. Opening my jaws, I add a volley of lighting. The metal spire explodes just as Zin and I fly through the spot.

Outside, the sight that greets us is a surprise. Everywhere we look, Triumvirate warriors stand in formation. Legion after legion stretch off to the horizon.

Moving as one, the soldiers raise their swords. For a moment, their blades waver.

Crash!

The legions collapse onto themselves. At every place where a warrior once stood, there's now a little pile of treasure.

"Guess we got him," says Zin.

"That we did." I'm about to suggest we fly a victory lap when it happens.

The explosions begin.

49

ZINNIA

*S*mash! Smash!

One by one, the mirrors surrounding the reflected realm of Abracadawn implode. A second ago, metal panels surrounded us. Now those appear as empty doorways. And what is visible beyond those many thresholds?

Earth.

Figures pour in through the new openings. I count Mum and Da, as well as a ton of Kathikon guard. Even Bash and Nikki are in the mix.

My Rhodes and I land before my parents. As we touch ground, both of us transform back to our human selves.

"Zinnia! Baby!" Mum wraps me in a hug.

"Little luv." Da gets in on the embrace as well. He looks over to my Rhodes. "Over here. That's an order."

My Rhodes joins in. For a long minute, we simply hold each other. I break the embrace.

"You did it," says Da. "Chimera is finally gone."

"How did you know?" I ask.

Mum grins. "I cast a ton of tracking spells on you two. I wanted to be sure you were safe, but then the spells came back that you'd destroyed Chimera."

"Give me details," says Da. "How ever did you manage it?"

If I live to be a thousand—and as a dragon, I very well may exist that long—I won't have many moments where I'm prouder than this one. "My Rhodes blasted him with lightning while I fried him with fire."

"Fire breathing!" Da pulls me in for another hug. "I knew you had it in you, little luv."

A Kathikon guard marches up. "Your Majesties, we found no signs of life here."

Mum looks to me. "Does that seem right?"

"Sadly, yes." I point to the great hole in the ground that once marked the silver spire. "Chimera's cave is down there. You'll find some bodies in there, but none living."

Da nods and focuses on the guard once ore. "Clean up the site and bring the bodies out."

"As you command." The guard marches away. Mum and Da step aside and whisper together. They do that a lot.

Nikki steps up. "Glad you're alive and all but … Do you see all this treasure around?"

"Take a pocketful or ten," says my Rhodes. "You've earned it."

Nikki beams. "I love my job!" She marches off and starts picking through the piles of gold and jewels.

Bash is next to approach us. "Good to see the pair of you alive."

"Would you like some treasure as payment?" I ask.

"I'll get something later," says Bash. "Right now, I'm just soaking in the whole *alternate reality* situation."

For Bash, that is an excessive amount of talking. I decide to let him have his moment.

Mum and Da approach us once more. Da raises his arms. "Attention! The empress and I have an announcement!"

Everyone falls silent.

If I thought my heart pounded away when Chimera was chasing me, it's nothing compared to what's happening now.

I've a pretty good idea what my parents are about to say.

RHODES

I set my hand on Zin's hip. Anticipation zings through every cell in my body.

Is this it? Can the moment really be here?

Empress Portia steps forward. "Rhodes and my daughter Zinnia have been through many adventures together. They created music as children. Later on, they found each other once more as adults. And now, they just defeated one of the worst threats to our land: Chimera."

Emperor Tempest moves to stand at Portia's side. "As a result, the empress and I agree. We hereby officially recognize Zinnia and Rhodes as rhanas. They are love bonded and may not be married to anyone else. We couldn't be happier."

Those words are like so many beams of sunlight into my heart. Taking Zinnia in my arms, I spin her about.

"This is it," I cheer. "We can truly be together."

ZINNIA

My Rhodes twists me until my head turns fuzzy. I can't find my balance; it's glorious.

For I have my Rhodes.

My love.

And although it all started with being dragged off by strangers and losing my Gracie, it now ends with a dizzy moment in my rhana's arms.

Perfection.

Thump, thump, thump.

The club's techno music blares. Lights flash. I wear leather short-shorts, a bandeau top and funky sneakers. I may want to blend in with the club goers, but a girl must be ready to run, too.

My cell buzzes against my hip. There's no need to check the device. No doubt, it's another text from Huntress, whining how I need to wait until she and Jade arrive.

Not going to happen.

The Wurtzite dagger is here.

I'm getting it.

I spy my target standing off to one side of the dance floor. He's a mountain of a guy with ink and muscles in worn jeans and black T-shirt. I scan him quickly. According to my source, he's got the dagger on him somewhere.

One way to find out.

I cross the room and pause before him.

"Hey," I say.

"Hi."

His chiseled face is far too handsome for his own good. A scar lines his chin, too. I am a sucker for someone who's been in a fight or two.

Now, I have my rules. *No emotions. No entanglements.* At this point, I could pinch a nerve on this guy and drop him like a sack of potatoes. Or I could dance with him a little and try to find out where he's hiding the dagger.

One little dance won't hurt.

Gripping his hands, I guide the man out onto the dance floor. He follows my lead. I also love a big dude who doesn't mind being led around a bit. It's hot.

All of which leads to another realization. Most big guys have the dance skills of a brick. But this one? He's got serious moves. There are some things he does with his hips that get me thinking. I've been saving myself. Not sure what for, but I'll know it when I see it. Maybe it's this man.

Stop it, Kaps.

No emotions. No entanglements.

After a few songs, my thigh is between his legs and we're grinding away to the beat of yet another song. He leans in and almost-not-quite kisses my neck. It's making me crazy.

The guy takes my hand and leads me off the dance floor. This would be the perfect moment to do that nerve-pinch move, but what can I say? I'm curious what he's planning.

We reach the back wall. The guy presses the emergency door open. An alarm blares for a few seconds, but the sound is barely audible over the club music. We step out into the relatively cool air of a back alley. Fortunately, it's a cute place: no stinky dumpsters or pee stains on the brickwork.

He flips me against the wall. My bare skin presses against the rough texture of brick. "I'll kiss you now."

"Please."

I have had my share of smooches. None of them compare to this. The guy does a full-body kiss. His left arm wraps about my shoulders; the right presses against the small of my back. His mouth plunders mine. He sets the rhythm and it's hypnotic. My mind hits a kind of lust trance.

Not so much that I forget about the dagger, though.

Reaching forward, I rub my hands over his chest and thighs. There's no sign of a dagger, but the looking-part is really enjoyable.

I slide my hands about his waist and that's when I hit it. A dagger is holstered at the base of his spine.

Yes.

This is familiar ground. I nip his lower lip. If you're lifting something from a mark's back, you need to distract him at another spot. *Lower lip biting* totally counts.

I pull the weapon free from its holster. Little by little, I circle my arm backward. I came prepared with holster along my spine. This bandeau top was specially made for these kind of jobs.

At this point, the outcome is pretty much set. I'll place the dagger in my own holster, tell the guy to buzz off, and be on my merry way. Only with this guy, that's almost a shame.

Almost.

I flip my hand behind my back, ready to reset the blade into its holster. That's when it happens.

The blade melts into tiny cords that wrap around my right wrist. Other metal lines swoop over to my left hand and bind me there as well.

"What the hell?" I ask.

"Hello, Princess," says the guy.

My legs turn a little wobbly. I lean against the wall. It's tempting to beat my head against it. I have rules for a reason. *No emotions. No entanglements.* Why did I dance with this m in the first place?

"Who are you?" I ask.

"Name's Mack. I'm a bounty hunter."

I try to process the words, but my head is turning fuzzy.

Bounty Hunter. That's not good.

"L'Griffe doesn't like how you've been picking on them. Gage asked me to bring you in."

Gage. That's the leader. "I'll fight you."

"You don't know how. And in about ten seconds tops, that metal will finish reacting with your shifter energy so you'll pass out."

If my legs were wobbly before, now they feel like nothing but wet noodles under me. My fuzzy head turns downright murky. I squint at Mack as I fight a losing battle to stay awake.

"But you kissed really well," I say.

"So did you, Princess."

Here's the thing. Mack has these searing blue eyes that seem to say, *I'm not lying about enjoying your kisses, even though I'm dragging you away to the evil shifter mafia.*

I open my mouth, ready to point out this very fact, when my legs finally give way. I'm taking a one-way trip to the pavement when my world turns entirely to black.

∾

—The End—

The adventure continues with Kaps, Book 5 of the Angelbound Offspring. Order now!

ALSO BY CHRISTINA BAUER

KAPS

The adventure continues with KAPS …

ANGELBOUND

Revisit ANGELBOUND, the kick-ass paranormal romance with more than 1 million copies sold!

LINCOLN

Enjoy Lincoln's perspective with the Angelbound LINCOLN series!

FAIRY TALES OF THE MAGICORUM

A modern fairy tale that *USA Today* calls a 'must-read!' Check out WOLVES AND ROSES!

DIMENSION DRIFT

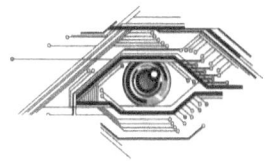

A kick-ass heroine + a swoon-worthy prince + an all-girl heist
= the DIMENSION DRIFT series!

BEHOLDER

Medieval mages … Slow-burn love … And heart-pounding action! Check out the BEHOLDER series!

PIXIELAND DIARIES

PIXIELAND DIARIES tells the story of sassy pixie Calla and 'her' elf prince, Dare.

Chapter One
KAPS

*S*ometimes, you simply must punch a shape-shifting vampire Nazi.

Like tonight, for instance.

I stroll through New York's Central Park. Ahead of me, there strides a guy in a chicken costume. I'm talking yellow feathers, plumed tail, the whole smash. A sash extends from his shoulder to his hip that reads *Eat At Cluck Town*. This fellow is anything but normal, and not for the obvious wardrobe reasons.

He's actually a vampire.

Even worse, he's an audax, which is a shape-shifting vampire Nazi. All audax started off as German soldiers in World War II. During a raid, they entered the magical city of El Dorado, got changed into vampires, and have been causing trouble ever since.

All of which is why I can't wait to punch this particular blood sucker.

With a stake.

Right through his heart.

Because I'm more than just a teenager who's dressed up for a night of dancing. I'm a dragon-shifter princess with a secret obsession.

Slaying audax.

I know. My life is strange. It runs in the family.

Squinting, I focus on the guy's birdy outfit. Dragon shifters like me are immune to supernatural glamours, so I can easily detect the decaying body that's magically hidden under all those feathers.

Hello, vampire.

The real costume-wearing human got attacked by an audax. After drinking the victim's blood, this particular vampire magically took on the man's appearance, bird outfit and all.

And the *original* chicken guy? Way dead.

Cold sorrow moves through me. Most likely, I'm the first to know about this lost life. I'm certainly the only one around here who detects the audax.

Ah, to be a clueless human. They've no idea how many evils surround them.

For his part, Vampire Chicken Guy (VCG for short) keeps sauntering along the stone path, his plumed tail bobbing with each step. He pulls off his fake chicken head to reveal someone my age—that would be seventeen—with round cheeks, short red hair and tons of freckles. *A stolen face.*

My grief melts into lava-hot rage. *How dare this audax kill a human?* I twist the clunky golden bracelet around my right wrist. If I take this off and flip the segments about, it transforms into a small spike. That's the only way to fully kill an audax...

A golden stake through the heart.

Meanwhile VCG smiles innocently at passersby. New Yorkers actually grin and wave in return, which is rare. *Must be a chicken thing.* I hoist up my bandeau top and keep following. The dance club can wait.

VCG is going down.

My prey slips off into a cluster of trees. Adrenaline courses through my bloodstream. Whipping off my bracelet, I convert the jewelry into a mini-stake. This size isn't as powerful as my regular weapon, but it'll get the job done. With every step, my tail sways behind me in a predatory rhythm. It's invisible to humans while being covered in dragon scales. *Super useful in a fight.*

I step into a small clearing—the same secluded nook that VCG just entered—and carefully scan my new surroundings.

There are trees.

Greenery.

And a random tortoise.

My heart sinks. No VCG.

Ring, ring...

I pull out my cell phone and see the familiar image of my sister, Huntress, on the screen. As always, Huntress carries an aristocratic air that says, *you shall follow me NOW.* It's her mix of fine features, violet eyes and oodles of confidence. By contrast, I have brown hair and eyes, as well as a vibe that screams, *I'm uncomfortable in my own skin.* Which is true.

Before answering, I take a moment to change character. Just now, I was playing the Lone Vigilante, a version of myself that fights vampires solo. When chatting with my sister, I must toss my Lone Vigilante self aside and become a new character, the Family Fuck Up. Because if folks knew about my Lone Vigilante antics, then I'd be locked up in a tower forever. No joke. My family's nutso when it comes to safety.

I pop in my earpiece. "Hey, Huntress."

"Ready for tonight's mission?"

A nearby shrub catches my attention. My Lone Vigilante instantly rises to the surface. *Maybe that shrub holds a clue about where VCG slunk off to.*

"Did you hear me?" asks Huntress.

"Uh, what was that again?" To play the Family Fuck Up, it's always important to stammer while asking dumbass questions.

"I was talking about tonight's mission," repeats Huntress. "Are you ready?"

A spot of yellow catches my eye. *Ah-HA!* That might be a feather. I step closer and indeed, I discover something colorful.

A Butterfinger wrapper. *Bummer.*

"Mission for what?" This time, I take care to imagine my head as full of cotton candy.

I can almost hear Huntress roll her eyes. "The Wurtzite dagger."

"Oh yeah. *That* mission."

Huntress clears her throat. "Here's the rundown for tonight, in case you forgot."

In other words, Huntress totally thinks I forgot.

In truth, I can recite every detail for tonight from memory. The Lone Vigilante forgets nothing.

"I'll start with the target," continues Huntress. "It's a

human male named Mack. Over six feet tall. Strong build. Blue eyes. Nineteen years old. Tonight he'll be carrying a Wurtzite dagger, which is a magical blade that can cut through anything."

Originally, Huntress and I needed the Wurtzite dagger to protect my twin, Zinnia. But Zin is totally safe these days. Now the Lone Vigilante wants the weapon because MAGICAL DAGGER.

Huntress keeps going. "According to my intel, Mack is due at La Vida tonight. Do you know the place?"

"Yup. I've hit that club before. Good dance spot."

"Oh, this is interesting," adds Huntress. "It says here, Mack is also part of the zoetic, a group of humans who fight something called the audax."

Now I could volunteer a ton of audax info at this point, but I won't. As far as my family is concerned, I'm a crackpot who loves touring Earth with my (arguably awful) rock band.

Yes, I'm living a lie. The rock band is just a cover. I only book gigs where there are vampires to kill or magical relics to uncover. And sure, it's kind of lonely. I juggle so many masks, I don't know which one is really me, if any.

At least I don't cry myself to sleep. I'm more of a *whimper and eat popcorn before bedtime* kind of girl.

A rustle sounds in the nearby trees. *Can that be VCG?* I pause.

Static crackles over my earpiece. "Do you know anything about the zoetic?" asks Huntress.

I step closer to the noisy tree. "One sec," I whisper.

"Hey," snaps Huntress. "Are you stalking someone?"

Wow. Leave it to Huntress to detect stalking behavior over the phone. She's well named, by the way. This girl can track anyone, anywhere.

"No, I'm just testing out this new…" I search for something that a fellow dragon shifter would believe. "Human exercise craze. You have to whisper while, uh, jogging."

Not my best lie.

"Exercise?" Huntress' voice takes on a decidedly skeptical note. "But you don't work out. Dragon shifters are naturally strong."

"Eh, you know me. Always trying crazy human stuff just for the fun of it."

"Oh." *And that's all Huntress needs to say.* My reputation as a nut job does the rest.

In the background, a palace servant asks something about a busted pipe. "Let me check," Huntress says to the servant. To me she asks: "Can you wait a sec?"

"No problem."

I tiptoe even closer to the tree. There's not much to see, unless you count bark and a few crawly things. By comparison, the Butterfinger wrapper seems like a great find. As a matter of fact, I'm about to give up the search when it happens.

VCG falls from the branches above.

And lands right on my head.

I get knocked to my stomach with a vampire chicken crouching on my back. Since his headgear is still off, the vamp leans in and licks my ear.

Eew.

"How fortunate that I shall kill you now," snarls the vampire. "If you sought out the Halcyon coven, then you'd die in a far more painful way."

Huh. In truth, I have zero plans to seek out the Halcyon witches. That said, I've always been interested in the Halcyons —mostly because they're somewhat related to the audax. And the fact that I'm being warned away from them?

Death be damned. Now I'm totally hunting the Halycons down.

After I kick this vampire's ass, obviously.

Chapter Two
MACK

I stand in a long stone room filled with cots. *The Zoetic Healing Chamber.* Small square windows line the walls, casting pale columns of light onto the floor. Three-hundred and four zoetic operatives lie here in neat rows. Every last of of them is unconscious.

None are healing.

We zoetic slay shape-shifting vampires. In our line of work, magical illnesses are a common risk. In the past, we've always healed from supernatural sickness.

Until a year ago. That's when the first zoetic fell ill into an enchanted sleep. And this isn't a magical snooze of the Snow White variety. Those who are struck down face a slow and painful death. All we can do is reduce their pain.

These days, our numbers are few. Zoetic who haven't fallen ill have run off. Not that I blame them. No one knows why zoetic are getting sick in the first place. Why hang around to be the next victim?

I scan the nearby cots. Familiar faces catch my attention.

There's Callista from our League of Bounty Hunters. Patariki the assassin. Mairwen of the Relic Masters. And Ndidi, the finest spy in our Cabal of Ghosts.

He's also my best friend.

I pause beside Ndidi's cot. Crimson mist shifts across his skin, clouding over his wide eyes, dark complexion and defined bone structure. It's this magical haze that keeps my friend asleep while it slowly takes his life.

Memories churn. I picture Ndidi and I training together as kids. Fighting side by side as adults. And always sharing a good laugh at bad jokes. Now I have no way to help him.

Bracing my shoulders, I wait for rage and sorrow to stab through me.

Nothing happens.

In truth, I haven't felt a twinge of feeling in months. Only emptiness. Ndidi warned me about this. He's always concerned for the welfare of others.

Pain is fire, Ndidi said. *If you aren't careful, it can burn out your soul.*

Seems he was right.

Our lead medic, Felix, steps up beside me. He's a stout guy in scrubs with unruly black hair and an easy smile. By contrast, I'm in my standard outfit: jeans and a black T.

"You never miss visiting hours, do you, Mako?" asks Felix.

"Try not to."

Actually, my name is Mack. The Mako nickname started six months ago, right when this hollowness settled into my heart. The fact that Felix calls me Mako—which is a type of shark—is meant as a complement. Other zoetic believe I'm a coldhearted predator who keeps going no matter what.

Felix lifts a small handheld from the pocket of his blue

scrubs. "I used the Spyglass of Tierney to check Ndidi last night." He flicks through some screens. "Your friend's bloom levels should be in here somewhere."

The bloom. That's what we call the rose-colored haze that keeps my friend in a magical sleep. It's a nice name for a horrific illness.

Felix is one hundred percent human, so he can't see the layers of crimson magic that move across Ndidi's body.

Yet I can.

There's a dash of demonic DNA in my heritage, so I detect the supernatural side of things without needing magical relics like the Spyglass of Tierney. Every day, I see stuff like demons, vampires and enchantments. In fact, I can even observe the worry tick that's gnawing on Felix's ear. It's a small demon that feeds off anxiety.

"Where *is* that screen?" Felix pulls on his earlobe, making the demon hop straight over his head, only to land on his other ear.

"You still have that worry demon."

Felix looks up, his eyes wide. "Are you sure?"

"Yeah." I crack my knuckles. "You want it gone? It won't hurt much."

Felix gasps. I shouldn't have said the *hurt much* part.

"No," replies Felix quickly. "I'm starting another herbal cleanse. This one will do the trick."

I shrug. I've already told Felix that you can't expel a worry tick without pain. But the medic has his own ideas.

Felix taps his screen. "Ah, here it is. There's hardly any bloom on Ndidi. Just a few spots here and there."

"Things have changed," I state, my voice low and calm. "The enchantment's all over him now. Ndidi's getting worse."

Felix pales. "And you aren't upset?"

"I am what you see." *Empty.*

Felix stares at me, his mouth hanging open with shock. "You really are a Mako."

He's not wrong. I gesture toward the data pad. "How about updating Ndidi's chart?"

"Sure, sure." Felix quickly types onto his data pad. Taking in a deep breath, the medic forces a smile. I've seen this move before. Felix wants to make some small talk and ease the situation. Not sure that's possible.

"You must be so excited," offers Felix.

"For what?"

"The other paladins."

Paladins like me have mastered all four zoetic orders: the League of Bounty Hunters, Order of Assassins, Relic Masters, and Cabal of Ghosts.

"Not sure what you mean."

"Next week, all the other paladins return from their retreat. Ace told me about it. You must be thrilled."

"Ace, right?" He's the only other paladin left. He also happens to be a scheming douchebag.

"Sure, Ace said the retreat was held in Scotland or something."

"Hmm."

Not sure what else to say. Truth is, there are no other paladins on retreat. It's just me and Ace these days—everyone else on our level is sick or run off.

"The paladins *do* return next week, right?" asks Felix.

The guy looks so hopeful, I can't be the one to burst his bubble. "Sure."

"Great news," says Felix. "See you later."

As Felix steps away, the main door to the healing chamber swings open. My Zoetic Liege, Roman, steps through. He's my height with a sinewy build. As always, Roman wears a white lab coat. He has unkempt gray hair, small round glasses, and a manic look in his silver eyes. Overall, he reminds me of a hyperactive Albert Einstein.

Roman raises his hand in greeting. "Eureka!"

I bow as he approaches. "My Liege."

"No formal nonsense today. I have found the cure for the bloom. Eureka!"

Roman often locks himself in his lab for weeks. By repeatedly saying *eureka,* my Liege means he has a new discovery to share. About half of these ideas are brilliant. The other fifty percent? *Ah, no.*

I fold my arms over my chest. "What is it?"

Roman grins. "We'll get the Essence."

Huh.

"Let me get this straight," I say slowly. "You'll cure the bloom by getting the Essence, which is a magical potion that can heal anything. Plus, the serum can only created by the Halcyon coven, a group of super-powerful witches who probably don't exist."

"Precisely! It's so simple and perfect, I don't know why I didn't see it before!"

That's Roman for you. One time, he wanted all zoetic to drink a potion so we could develop a third eye. Literally.

Roman pulls some crumpled documents from the pocket of his lab coat. "Remember that vial Ace found last month?"

"From the Black Lotus coven. It was all dried out. Maybe a drop of potion left?"

"That's the one." Roman presses the papers into my hands.

"It's all in these documents. I reconstituted the liquid. The Black Lotus didn't brew that serum. The magical signature says Halcyon."

I scan the analysis in my hands, which resembles nothing more than a mishmash of letters. But if you read every fifth one, the words become clear. I read them aloud. "Property of the Halcyon coven." I lift my brows. "I'll be damned."

"And look what this potion does." Roman shoves more pages in my direction.

I inspect the new sheets. In these tests, just a fraction of a droplet eats through almost any pathogen. "Wow. This serum *does* act like the Essence."

"The Halcyons are real. So is the Essence. No one's better at uncovering supernatural artifacts than you, Mack. You'll soon discover a magical relic that leads to both the Halcyons and the Essence. I know it."

"All right, Roman." I set my hand on his shoulder. "I'll try."

With that, I saunter off, cell phone in hand. In cases like this, there's only one group to call.

The dragon shifter mafia.

∼

—The End—

The adventure continues with Kaps, Book 5 of the Angelbound Offspring. Order now!

APPENDIX

.

IF YOU ENJOYED THIS BOOK...

...Please consider leaving a review, even if it's just a line or two. Every bit truly helps, especially for those of us who don't *write by the numbers,* if you know what I mean.

Plus I have it on good authority that every time you review an indie author, somewhere an angel gets a mocha latte. For reals.

And angels need their caffeine, too.

ACKNOWLEDGMENTS

If you're reading my freaking acknowledgements, chances are, I should thank you for something. So, for the record: you are awesome, dear reader.

That said, huge and heartfelt thanks must go out to my husband and son for their rock-solid support. Being an author means a lot of early mornings, late nights, long weekends, and never-ending patience. You two are the best guys in the universe, period.

After that, I must thank the extensive network of reviewers, friends and colleagues who helped me build my writing chops in general. Gracias.

Finally, deep affection goes out to my late, much loved, and dearly missed Aunt Sandy and Uncle Henry. You saw the writer in me, always. Thank you, first and last.

ABOUT CHRISTINA BAUER

Christina Bauer thinks that fantasy books are like bacon: they just make life better. All of which is why she writes romance novels that feature demons, dragons, wizards, witches, elves, elementals, and a bunch of random stuff that she brainstorms while riding the Boston T. Oh, and she includes lots of humor and kick-ass chicks, too. Christina lives in Newton, MA with her husband, son, and semi-insane golden retriever, Ruby.

Stalk Christina on Social Media

Blog:
http://monsterhousebooks.com/blog/category/christina

Facebook:
https://www.facebook.com/authorBauer/

Instagram:
https://www.instagram.com/christina_cb_bauer/

Twitter:
@CB_Bauer

VLOG:
https://tinyurl.com/Vlogbauer

Web site:
www.bauersbooks.com

COMPLIMENTARY BOOK

Get a FREE novella when you sign up for Christina's newsletter: https://tinyurl.com/bauersbooks

BEVERLY HILLS VAMPIRE

A NOVELLA BY CHRISTINA BAUER

www.ingramcontent.com/pod-product-compliance
Lightning Source LLC
Chambersburg PA
CBHW031955170626
46807CB00006B/2495